side effects

A Deborah Brodie Book

ROARING BROOK PRESS

New Milford, Connecticut

AMY GOLDMAN KOSS

side effects

A Deborah Brodie Book
Published by Roaring Brook Press
Roaring Brook Press is a division of
Holtzbrinck Publishing Holdings Limited Partnership
143 West Street, New Milford, Connecticut 06776

Library of Congress Cataloging-in-Publication Data
Koss, Amy Goldman
Side effects / Amy Goldman Koss.— 1st ed.
p. cm.
"A Deborah Brodie Book."
Summary: Everything changes for Isabelle, not quite fifteen,
when she is diagnosed with lymphoma—but eventually she
survives and even thrives.
ISBN-13: 978-1-59643-294-9
ISBN-10: 1-59643-294-2
[1. Cancer—Fiction. 2. Chemotherapy—Fiction.
3. Family problems—Fiction.] I. Title.
PZ7.K8527Sid   2006   [Fic]—dc22
2005   031473
10 9 8 7 6 5 4 3 2 1

Roaring Brook Press books are available for special
promotions and premiums. For details, contact:
Director of Special Markets, Holtzbrinck Publishers.

Book design by Robin Hoffmann / Brand X Studios
Printed in the United States of America
First edition September 2006

Also by
AMY GOLDMAN KOSS

Poison Ivy

you go along, minding your own business (more or less), then *BAM!* You win the lottery, a piano falls on your head, you're struck by lightning and fried to a crisp. Or, like Izzy Miller, your plain old swollen glands turn out to be a kind of cancer you never even heard of before. From that second on, everything and everyone around you gets weirder than weird, and your only choice is to push through it—or in Izzy's case, *puke* through it—and try to stay sane.

And, as if it doesn't suck enough to have cancer, practically every time you pick up a book or see movies where characters get sick, you know they'll be dead by the last scene.

In reality, kids get all kinds of cancers, go through unspeakable torture and painful treatments, but walk away fine in the end.

This book is about that descent into hell, with a safe return. I dedicate it to everyone who has been there and back.

deepest heartfelt gratitude to the amazing staff at Children's Hospital, Los Angeles, especially Sherri Carcich, RN, care manager for the Leukemia and Lymphoma Program, and Dr. Anna Butturini, director of the ABMT Program, Center for Cancer and Blood Diseases, Children's Hospital, Los Angeles.

{ ONE }

the overhead light snapped on and my shoulder got one quick shake. Pupkin, who hated the morning wars, jumped off my bed, leaving a cold spot. He followed Mom, his toenails clicking down the hall.

I grabbed a moment of peace until my mother returned to poke me in the ribs in a totally obnoxious way that started the hate stirring. Was that any way to begin a day, with stirring hate and the light burning through my eyelids?

But that's Mom's style, a series of quick, hostile advances, retreats, and repeats to annoy her victim into wakefulness, like a human mosquito. I had to sleep braced for the next attack. And there she was, yanking off my blankets. *Hey!*

With swearing from me, ragging from Mom, and snarling from both of us, I stumbled to the shower. What was left of the hot water felt great, but then it was gone, thanks to my little brother, Max.

I wiped the steam off the mirror, to see what needed plucking or squeezing, trying to see myself through Jared Peterson's incredible baby-blue eyes. But something looked weird.

I wrapped myself in a towel and called, *"Mom!"*

"What?"

"Come here."

"Can't now. What?"

"No, really. Look."

She came, grumbling, "You're late again, and there's no way I've got time to drive you. You'll just have to—"

I cut her off and pointed to the mirror. She glanced at my reflection, cloudy with steam.

"Look at my neck; my glands are still sticking out. That flu was *ages* ago."

She peered closer at the mirror, then at me. "I'll call Dr. Posner, see if he can fit you in today. Now get dressed and get going. It's almost seven." Then she went back to the kitchen to yell at my brother for something.

second hour I was in Drama class. A girl, Nina, was reading her sonnet with way too much emotion. I was drawing a picture of her for my friend Kay, who couldn't draw worth shit and thought every doodle I doodled was brilliant.

Just as I was putting sweat beads on Nina's brow, a voice came through the speaker telling Ms. Blaire to send me to the office with my belongings.

Nina crossed her arms in a huff at the interruption. She tapped her foot in irritation as I shut my notebook and slid it into my backpack. I was tempted to move in extra slow motion just to see how many times I could get her to roll her eyes.

Kay mouthed the question, "Where're you going?"

I shrugged. Half the time when kids were pulled out of class it was to go to the orthodontist. The other half was because their grandparents had died. But I didn't have braces or grandparents.

My mom was in the office, signing me out. I saw her write *doctor's appointment* and I remembered my swollen glands. I touched my neck—they were still there. Good! If the doctor's office was crowded enough, this could eat up half the day.

In the car, Mom asked the usual: "How was school?"

"Fabulous."

She perked up. "Really?"

"It sucked, Mom. It always sucks."

"Please don't use that word."

"Which word?"

Mom sighed.

Traffic stopped to let a fat woman wearing a green garbage bag push her shopping cart across the street. It was hot out and she must've been sweltering in that outfit, plus the asphalt had to be hell on her bare feet. Someone leaned on his horn to either speed the bag lady up or encourage the guy who'd stopped for her to run her down.

"Butt-wad," I murmured.

Mom looked at me, then looked closer. "I wish you'd worn a nicer shirt," she said. She reached over to scrape some breakfast off my sleeve. If I'd let her, she would've scrubbed it with her spit.

Then we were in Posner's waiting room with a little kid throwing a very impressive tantrum. His mom's solution was to keep pointing at the aquarium, saying "See the pretty fishies?" in a very high, very irritating, very fake voice.

Why do people squeak like that at children? Is there some scientific reason? Or is it just to make sure that all kids grow up to despise and distrust their elders?

Another woman was nursing what appeared to be a blanket. There were a lot of sloppy, slurpy noises.

I was definitely too old to be there. The whole waiting room was full of baby stuff and *Highlights* magazines and chewed-up Dr. Seuss books.

I'd left my notebook and everything in the car, or I might have done a drawing of that weird wire thing with the colored beads, which exists only in doctors' waiting rooms. I wondered what was supposed to be *fun* about it. All I'd ever wanted to do was get the beads *off* the damn thing so I could play with them. Maybe that toy—if you can even call it a toy—was meant to teach frustration and hopelessness. *Hey, kids! Feeling sick? Scared of the doctor? Well, here are some beads you can't have! Ha-ha!*

Mom was chatting up the nursing mother. Why she always has to do that, I do *not* know. Mom was telling her something insanely boring about my infancy, or my brother's, and I practically wished I was back in school—but not quite.

Then Dora, who I actually *didn't* hate, took us to examining room 4. She asked me why I was there. Mom answered, "Swollen glands."

Dora asked if I'd had a sore throat or fever. Mom said no.

Dora asked me how long my glands had been swollen, and if they hurt. Mom answered the best she could.

Dora told me to hop up on the examining table. I half expected Mom to jump up there for me.

Dora said the doctor would be with us soon, but I didn't hold it against her for lying. Maybe she was an optimist and really believed that *this* time, Dr. Posner would make it into the room before I died of boredom.

Mom pointed to the baby scale, like she always does, and told me I used to *hate* being weighed.

I said, "I know."

She looked at the *Sesame Street* books, and I knew she wished I'd sit on her lap and let her read one to me.

"Do you think I'll get a shot?" I asked. I hated shots. The worst part about a shot was the *idea* of a shot, but knowing that the worst part was the idea didn't make the idea any less horrible.

"Oh, Izzy, shots aren't so bad," Mom said. "Stings for a second, then it's over."

She wasn't going to get anyone to sit on her lap and listen to Big Bird stories with *that* kind of sympathy.

The crinkly paper on the examining table stuck to my thighs. I asked Mom if she thought they recycled it. "You figure they roll out a fresh three or four feet for each patient," I said. "That's a lot of paper. They could donate it to schools for art projects."

Mom wrinkled her nose. "That wouldn't be very sanitary," she said.

I nodded. "You're right. There'd be skid marks from all those itty-bitty ass holes."

"Don't swear, Izzy, please," Mom said automatically.

Many years later, Dr. Posner came in and made a few lame jokes, which Mom laughed at, not because they were funny, but so Posner would doctor me well. Then he asked why I was there.

I wondered if Dora knew that he paid zero attention to the notes she took, day after day, patient after patient.

As soon as he had re-asked all Dora's questions, he felt my neck. "It's probably mononucleosis. Or, as it's commonly called," he told us commoners, "mono. But we'll have Dora take a TB test for good measure. Then

I'd like you to run across the street to the hospital for a chest X-ray."

Hmmm. My pediatrician was suggesting that I *run* across the street?

But, cool. The hospital always takes forever, so for sure it'd be too late to go back to school afterward. I wondered if Jared would notice I wasn't in History.

When Dora came back in with the TB test, I scooted off the table and sat next to my mom. I scrunched my face into her shoulder, closed my eyes, stuck out my arm, held my breath, and squeezed Mom's hand while Dora stabbed me.

Dora teased that she'd seen braver five-year-olds and toddlers with higher pain tolerance. Nonetheless, she gave me a Hello Kitty sticker, as always.

as far as the hospital taking all day, I must've been thinking about the *emergency room* the time my brother, Max, got hit by a baseball or the time he fell off the skate ramp or when he burned himself so mysteriously or when he drove a nail through his finger. This was different. The radiology department was nowhere near the emergency room, and they took me in immediately.

Mom talked to everyone there, of course.

The Filipino X-ray guy with a tattoo of a lion peeking out under his sleeve moved me around in front of the X-ray machine. His hands were warm through my thin hospital gown. He said something about being Superman, seeing through me, and it's entirely possible that I blushed.

Mom and I waited around for him to make sure the X-ray had worked. But when he came back to tell me I could get dressed, he was no longer smiling or flirty.

"Your doctor will call you at home" was all he said, so I figured he didn't like me anymore.

On the way back to the car, Mom asked what time my lunch hour was. I asked, "Why?"

"Because if you missed it, we can pick you up something."

I didn't like the sound of that. "I'll eat at home," I said.

"It's only twelve twenty," Mom said. "There's still almost half the school day left, and I've got to get back to the office." Mom didn't look at me; I guess she could imagine my scowl.

"Please don't make me go back, Mom," I begged. "After all that. Posner, then the X-rays. And nothing's happening today, I swear."

Mom sighed, which in this instance meant I'd won.

She called her office and told John she'd see him tomorrow. Then we went to the Toasted Bun. My omelet was extra delicious since I was supposed to be in Algebra.

"Mono is called the kissing disease, you know," Mom said, extracting the tomatoes from her salad.

Humph, I grunted, mouth full of toast.

"So, who've you been kissing?"

"Just Pupkin," I said. "Well, Pupkin, and this very nice old guy who offered me a lollipop if I'd get in his car."

"Izz, I'm serious," Mom said.

"Me too," I replied.

Mom sighed, again.

It's so unfair, I thought, that I should get a kissing disease without first getting the kissing. Of course, if you could get a kissing disease from hours spent fantasizing, I'd be a goner. Like the bus ride home from the Science field trip. I'd nabbed the seat next to Jared without, I thought, seeming too obvious. We'd talked a little to each other, but what felt even better was talking to the kids all around us, as if we were one voice. *He and I* talked to them—and I felt all this couplelike we-ness.

A while later, I pretended to fall asleep. I'm a tiny bit taller than Jared, so I had to scoot down to let my head fall accidentally on his shoulder. After a while, he very, very gently rested his head on mine, and it was unbelievably fabulous. A head-hug. My leg hummed, lined up against Jared's, communicating in sex-speak. Every one of my deliriously horny skin cells was practically screaming to every one of his, without a sound. It was so cosmic I could hardly breathe.

I knew that he knew that I wasn't really sleeping and that, any second, we'd turn our faces to each other and we'd kiss and it would be unbelievable. The suspense was murder.

Then Jared snored himself awake. "Oh, man," he laughed, shaking himself, "I guess I passed out." Then he turned around to talk to the kids behind us, leaving a cooling puddle of drool on my arm.

The whole steamy scene had been in my head.

Now I wondered what—if anything—Jared would think when he heard I had mono. Would he be even a tiny bit jealous that maybe I'd been kissing *someone*?

since she was off from work anyway, Mom figured this would be a good time to pick up the dry cleaning and run fifty other errands. By the time we got home, it was practically as if I'd been in school all day. I couldn't bring myself to start my homework or else I'd have gotten *nothing* extra out of this at all.

When I checked the clock, it said I still had twenty-five minutes to kill before Kay got out of class and I could call her. That's how I knew it was 2:05 when the phone rang.

My mom answered, and I didn't think anything of it until I heard the strangest moan. An animal kind of moan that made me think Pupkin was hurt. Then I heard Mom's voice, but low and groaning, go, "Noooo. Oh no. Oh no." I ran to the kitchen, terrified.

Mom was on the floor, with her legs sprawled. She was slumped against the counter as if she'd slid down. She looked unnatural and uncomfortable, with the phone still in her hand. The scene was weird, but Pupkin was safe and sound, licking Mom's face. I nearly laughed, but then I thought, Shit! Someone's hurt! Or dead! Dad? Max?

But it was me.

Mom delivered the news from down there. And, as if that wasn't surreal enough, the news she had to deliver was beyond sense. "That was Dr. Posner," she said in a weird, moany voice. "He told me to take you to Children's Hospital right away. Today. Now." She looked up from the floor with a confused frown and said, "He said you have lymphoma."

"Lymphoma? What the hell is *lymphoma*?" I asked. And I knew it was serious because Mom didn't tell me not to swear. Her eyes were huge. She didn't get up.

"Mom!" I yelled. "What's lymphoma?"

"He said they have much better luck with it now," she answered, if you can call that an answer. Then she auto-dialed my aunt Lucy, and I heard her say, "Lou? They think Isabelle has cancer. Meet us at Children's Hospital. We're going now," and she hung up.

They thought I had *what*? Then I was on the floor too, as if all my bones had either melted or been suddenly removed.

if the cancer didn't kill me, the ride to the hospital would. Mom's eyes were streaming tears and she was babbling first into the phone at my dad, then just babbling in general. I watched LA go by outside the window and marveled that everything looked so normal. There was the *Live Nude Girls* sign that made me wonder, when I was little, whether other places had *dead* nude girls. We crossed the Los Angeles River, which was just a dribble of scum between graffiti-covered concrete banks.

We had never been to Children's before. We could see it now, sticking up over the shorter buildings around it—a Blockbuster, a gas station, a thrift store with a blue '50s prom dress in the window.

Mom wasn't sure where the parking lot was.

A homeless guy and his dalmatian sat on the curb in front of the public TV station, where we stopped for a red light. His sign said, *Good karma 1 dollar. OK karma, fifty cents.*

I pointed him out to my mom and she grabbed a handful of ones from her purse and frantically waved them at the man, calling, "Yoo-hoo!"

The light changed. The guy had trouble standing up. Cars behind us honked, so Mom crunched up the bills and threw them. Poor guy was going to have to dodge traffic to pick them up off the street.

I wanted to call Kay, but as bizarre as it seemed, it was *still* too early. How weird, that I'd be in History, scribbling on my folder, sneaking peeks at blue-eyed Jared, and thinking about whatever it is I thought about when I wasn't on my way to Children's Hospital with cancer.

"Mom?" I asked, interrupting her chatter. "Will I lose my hair?"

"Does that say 'patient parking' or what?" she asked, pointing to a sign. "Should I go in there?"

I shrugged.

"They said *bed*," Mom muttered. "They'd have a *bed* ready. So a parking meter won't be long enough, right? I'd have to keep feeding it quarters all night or I'd get a ticket. Would they ticket a hospital? A *children's* hospital?"

Tears slid down her face, getting sidetracked by wrinkles and divided into streams. There were no crying noises, thank God.

Bed? Hospital bed? That's where I was going to sleep? How much sense did *that* make?

the lobby of this hospital was nothing like the one we'd been in that morning. This one was big and bright and decorated to look *fun*. Who did they think they were kidding?

People were everywhere. Carrying babies. Pushing strollers and wheelchairs. Kids wearing surgical masks. Lots of fat people in tight clothes. I let Mom take my arm.

Then Aunt Lucy came charging up and scooped us into a hug. Mom burst into noisy sobs to go with her tears. I extracted myself from Mom's juicy clutches and looked out the window at a pretty little garden. I wondered if that was where they took people to tell them their kids were dead.

"Okay!" My aunt barked at Mom. "You've had your cry. Now suck it up. Do you hear me?"

Mom nodded, but the tears kept flowing. Aunt Lucy led Mom to the Admissions desk and pushed her into a chair. "This is Isabelle Miller's mother," my aunt told the lady working there.

Then she turned to my mom and said, "Answer the questions, Helen. Izzy and I are going to the gift shop," and she swept me away, leaving Mom looking scared and damp.

Aunt Lucy doesn't have any daughters, or sons, either, for that matter. So I'm the one she's always telling her funeral plans to, even though she's only forty-three. Sometimes she tells me she wants to be buried facedown so the world can kiss her ass good-bye. Sometimes she wants to be cremated and her ashes spread on Rodeo Drive in Beverly Hills, or the Paseo Mall in Old Town, Pasadena, at the ritzy shoe stores.

"You better kill yourself right now, if you still want me to arrange your funeral," I said, mostly kidding. "Looks like I won't be here to do it later."

"Not funny," my aunt answered. "And don't go making any death-jokes around your mother, Isabelle, or I will personally kill you."

The hospital gift shop had no shoes, but it was full of pink, blue, and purple fairies. And there were fairy princess crowns and charms and wands streaming pink ribbons and stars.

"Everything here is for little girls. Don't boys get sick?" my aunt asked the lady behind the counter.

The woman put her hand to her chest as if she were afraid we'd steal her VOLUNTEER badge.

Aunt Lucy whirled around in the tiny shop. "Izzy," she barked, getting my drifty attention away from a gaudy jewelry box that had hypnotized me. "Magazines?"

I shook my head no.

"Stuffed animal?"

I rolled my eyes and hoped she was kidding.

They had crayons and paint sets, but I wasn't into color. I only liked to draw with Paper Mate blue-ink, medium-point pens on lined paper. I looked for a spiral notebook but didn't see one.

Aunt Lucy pointed to a jigsaw puzzle of kittens with bows.

As if.

"Then we're outta here," she said, and whisked me back to where my mom sat like a lost-looking lump.

We were given directions: Turn right, turn left, take the giraffe elevators, whatever. I wasn't listening. Mom clutched my sleeve and tried to lead me, but Aunt Lucy, always the big sister, spun her around and marched us the other way.

Each elevator was a different animal—tiger, peacock, and giraffe. "This could turn kids off the animal kingdom for keeps," I said.

Aunt Lucy smiled. Mom just stared through her tears.

The elevator doors opened on a little kid, maybe seven or eight, without a single hair on its head. Without hair, it's hard to tell boys from girls at that age. Jeans and tees are jeans and tees. The kid had a huge, stitched-up gash across his/her skull.

Mom let out a mammoth, moany sigh.

I elbowed her to shut up.

{ TWO }

the fourth floor was yellow. A long, wide hall, strange machinery parked here and there, nurses and orderlies hurrying along. Other people stood in tight clumps. One huge baby in a nightgown was pushing a miniature of itself in a stroller. They looked like twins. But then I realized the kid was probably fourish; she just looked like a baby because she was as bald as her doll.

It would've made an interesting drawing.

A pretty nurse asked me if I was Isabelle. She acted glad to see me, as if she'd been waiting just for me. She had a little accent of some sort and her shoes squeaked as she led us down the hall. Peeking into each room we passed, I saw beds, kids, some alone, some with grown-ups hovering.

The nurse told me her name, but it flew right out of my head. I tried to keep up with her, listening to what she was saying. Something about it being a madhouse. "Many people are going to come and talk to you over the next few hours," she said. "A lot of information will be thrown your way. Don't worry if some slips by; if it's important, it'll come back around."

She said she'd be glad to answer any questions I had, and I shouldn't be afraid of sounding stupid.

By this time, she'd taken us into a dim room and patted a bed. There was a curtain around it, half-pulled, so I couldn't see what was on the other side.

I sat where she'd patted.

She put a white plastic bracelet on my wrist, then said, "First off, we have to get an IV started. 'IV' is short for 'intravenous,' meaning 'in the vein,'" she said. "As you probably know."

That's where I almost lost it. An IV? In me? That would be even more *shot* than a shot. I looked at my mom and my aunt, huddled at the foot of my bed, their four eyes blinking like two owls. There was no one to help me.

"I just have to get my supplies," the nurse said. "Did you bring a nightie or do you need a hospital gown?"

I looked back at Mom.

"Oh!" she said, pulling out her phone, "I'll tell Daddy to bring pajamas."

But the nurse stopped her. "Sorry," she said, "you can't use cell phones here. They interfere with some of the life-saving equipment."

Mom dropped her phone as if it were on fire.

The pretty nurse said, "I'll be right back," and left.

Aunt Lucy whipped out a notepad and scribbled *PJs*. The pad was small but better than nothing. Her pen was the kind that clicks up and down, and the ink was black, but, oh well.

"Can I have that?" I asked my aunt.

She held up her notepad "This?"

"Yeah, and your pen," I said. "Unless you've got one with blue ink."

"How can you think about ink now?" Mom asked, looking genuinely baffled.

Aunt Lucy ripped off the page she'd written on and gave me the rest. Then she rummaged for a blue pen. Nope.

I clicked her black-ink pen in and out and looked around at my nightstand, my table thing, and the TV, up near the ceiling. I wondered if those things ever came crashing down during earthquakes. There was a mail-box-looking slot in the wall that said *Hazardous Waste Materials.* It had a skull and crossbones on it. Nice.

Then I saw the phone and dived for it. "Can I call Kay?" I asked. Mom looked around, as if afraid we'd get in trouble. My aunt said, "Of course." Then they both continued to stand practically on top of me.

"Do you mind?" I asked. They got the hint, but backed off only a fraction of an inch.

Whatever. I held the phone on my shoulder and started to doodle. When Kay answered, I said, "Guess where I am?" But then I didn't have the patience to let her guess, so I said, "I'm in Children's Hospital. I have cancer."

"Funny," Kay said. Then she started to tell me I'd missed seeing Tara Hutchinson all over Brad Dowel on the bus on the way home, and how Claudia acted like she didn't care, although everyone knew it must've been eating her alive.

"I'm not kidding," I said. "Remember those swollen glands I had?"

I did a quick drawing of them sticking out like tree branches from my neck, like Pinocchio's nose after a whopping lie. I drew a vulture perched on one. Not that I'd ever seen a vulture, except in cartoons.

A different nurse walked in and stood at the side of my bed.

"Hang on a sec," I told Kay. I asked the nurse if she wanted me. She nodded. This nurse wasn't as cute as the first one, but she carried a basket with a white stuffed animal in it. I thought it was a poodle, but maybe not. I figured she was bringing me a *welcome to the hospital* gift. I didn't want to be rude and tell her I wasn't the stuffed-animal type, so I smiled.

I told Kay I had to go.

But it wasn't a present. It was a decoy! A trick! That nurse was there to take my *blood*. The white stuffed animal was just hiding the needles and test tubes in her basket.

I let Mom give me her hand to squeeze while the nurse stabbed me. I didn't know if those were Mom's *my daughter's in the hospital* tears, or tears from my squeezing so hard. The nurse filled vial after vial with my beautiful blood. I was sorry to see it go.

The first nurse returned with a machine that she plugged into the wall. She turned knobs and the machine made noises. Meanwhile, another woman came in wearing a whole bunch of necklaces tangled with her ID badge around her neck. She introduced herself as my oncologist, but she pronounced it funny, with a fabulous Jamaican accent. Her sidekick was an intern who looked like she was my little brother's age.

A baby was wailing in the background while the oncologist told me not to eat because I was having a biopsy in the morning. She also told me that the surgeon and the anesthesiologist would be along to meet me sometime in the next few hours. All their names blurred.

My hand kept busy, shading the Pinocchio-swollen-gland drawing, putting feathers on the vulture and saliva dripping from its beak. Do vultures have saliva?

My dad peered into the room as if afraid of what he'd find there. Then he saw me and rushed in to give me a dad-hug. "Izzy-pie, Izzy-pie," he whispered, his beard tickling my forehead. "This is no place for my Izzy-pie."

Mom introduced him to the doctor and the intern. Dad got it together and shook their hands. Mom crept over to cling to Dad's jacket, and they pretended to listen to the Jamaican oncologist spout numbers and statistics. Normally, my dad was a sucker for facts and figures, but I could tell from the look on his face that none of this was sinking in.

Aunt Lucy was busily taking notes, though, on the one sheet of paper I'd let her keep. Maybe if she read it to us later, it would make some sense.

the oncologist and her little pal left, but crowds of other strangers came in and surrounded me, until Nurse Number One shooed everyone out and pulled the curtain around my bed. "I've brought you two hospital gowns," she said, "so you can put one on backward and one frontward and nothing will hang out anywhere."

I thanked her, and she left me to change.

I was alone on my island in this strange new sea of medical weirdness. I closed the tiny notebook and clipped Aunt Lucy's black pen to the cover. Then I took off my jeans but didn't know what to do with them. I wadded them up and jammed them to the foot of my bed. Should I take off my underwear? Should I get under the covers like I was sick, even though I felt fine and it was probably only, like, four o'clock?

Actually, I had no idea what time it was. I didn't even know if it was dark out. I wished Pupkin were there, curled up warm next to me.

"Knock-knock!" said the pretty nurse, and she stuck her head through the curtain. "Ready?"

Ready to have an IV needle jabbed into me? No. "What's in there, anyway?" I asked.

"In the IV? Water, to keep you from getting dehydrated, and glucose, to give you calories for energy."

"So it's fattening?" I asked.

"Let's see your arm," the nurse answered.

I held out both. I still had a smiley-face Band-Aid from Dora's TB test all those years ago at Posner's. And the sneaky bloodsucker with the poodle decoy had left a cotton ball taped to the inside of my elbow.

The nurse examined my smiley arm closely. Then she looked at the other one. She thumped and pressed. "Tiny veins," she said.

"Is that a compliment or an insult?" I asked.

"Are those my only choices?" She smiled. "How about just a statement of fact, with no value judgment?"

"In other words, it's an insult," I said.

And she laughed.

Mom crawled in under the curtain and sat on the foot of my bed. She folded my jeans and shirt and held them on her lap. Her eyes were red and puffy, making her look like a ninety-year-old version of herself.

I grabbed Mom's hand. The nurse swabbed my arm with red stuff, then asked if I wanted her to count.

I shrugged and scrunched my eyes shut.

She said, "One... two..." Then on "three," she stabbed the needle in one side of my arm and out the other. I broke three of my mother's fingers, but all I said was "Ouch."

The nurse, who looked considerably less cute now, armed with that syringe, said, "Sorry, we have to try again." She told me to take a deep breath and let it out on *three*. "Ready? One . . . two . . . *out!*" First there was the stab, then she started twisting the needle around in my arm, digging for the vein.

The nurse pulled out the needle a second time and rechecked my other arm to see if my veins were any better there.

"The third time's the charm!" she said cheerfully, going for the tender inside of my elbow. I tried not to hate her.

The third time was *not* the charm, so a different nurse came to try while the first one patted my head. I hate having my head patted.

I kept my cool, but Mom's face was a mirror of how I really felt. It reminded me of a story we read in English last year called *The Picture of Dorian Gray*, about this guy who stayed young and sweet-looking even though he kept doing shitty things. Meanwhile, his secret portrait got older and uglier instead of him. Mom was my portrait.

Soon I had three different nurses discussing my veins. They told me and my mom that I should have a PICC line put in if I was going to need chemotherapy. "Then she won't have to have so many needle sticks," one nurse said. Another explained that they'd put it in while I was in surgery tomorrow for my biopsies.

Until then, I hadn't really understood that I was going to get *surgery*. Or that something like *chemotherapy* could possibly have anything to do with *me*.

They said the PICC line was a permanent line that would give them access to my vein whenever they needed to either take blood or administer medicines.

Considering I'd lived the first fourteen and a half years of my life without ever needing *access* to my veins, I thought they were just talking crazy.

Then they said someone would come around later to give us lessons on how to flush the PICC line and keep it clean at home.

"*Home?* Let me get this straight," I said. "You'd leave a tube in me, with, like, a *cork* in it, and I'm supposed to muck around with it myself?"

All three nurses nodded. The head-patter said, "You have to clean it daily to avoid infection."

I looked at each of them, to see if they were serious. "Are you saying I'd wear this tube *home?* Like, have an open tube in my arm all the time? At school even?"

"In your chest, actually," a nurse with dreadlocks said. "But it sounds worse than it is. Really. Your clothes will cover it."

"Eeew," I said. "That's possibly the grossest thing I've ever heard." I looked around for Aunt Lucy's notepad and pen.

The ex-pretty nurse said, "We'll think about that later. For now, we've got to get this IV started." And they had another go at me, this time stabbing near my wrist. Everyone cheered when my blood backed up into the syringe. Great.

Someone just outside my door was talking with my dad and aunt. I could make out only occasional words. But two of the words were *PICC line*.

"I don't want it!" I called out to them. "No PICC line!"

My dad popped his head in to see what I was yelling about.

"I do *not* want the PICC line!" I said. "I'm serious."

Dad said, "But they say, in the long run—"

I cut him off. "No! I'm *not* wearing tubes to school!"

Meanwhile, one of the nurses said, "The PICC line makes it a lot easier for us. And it would mean fewer sticks for you."

I grumbled at her, and she smiled. "But you do have the right to say no," she said. "It's your body."

"Damn right it is!" I said. And she smiled again. I liked her. Meanwhile, she'd been taping the needle in place. And taping my whole hand to a board the size and shape of a Kotex, so I wouldn't bend my wrist and spurt blood all over. Out of this mess snaked a tube that led up to a plastic bag of clear liquid on a pole. There was a square machine on the pole that ticked like a time bomb.

I imagined calling Jared. Going, *Hi, Jared. It's Izzy. The girl with the hots for you in History? I'm calling from my hospital bed, and I just wanted to say . . . farewell.* How could he resist that? It would be so damn romantic!

I was now down to just one nurse—pushing buttons on my time bomb, so I thought we were done. But she said no, she had to put me on a cardiac monitor.

"A *what?*" I said.

She laughed as if I were joking.

So much for modesty. The next thing I knew, she reached inside my hospital gown to stick little science-fiction electrode things all over my chest.

"There's a room down the hall on your right," she said, adding wires to my back, "with games and puzzles and books and videos that you're welcome to borrow, or use there, anytime you like. And Friday's pizza."

Big Whoop! I thought. But then, *Friday?* Today was only Tuesday! Hey! I have a History test Friday. So at least there's *that*. I mean, who could expect me to study for a History test while I'm being impaled with needles and wired to machines?

"Nothing for my brain?" I asked. "No metal helmet with lightning bolts to complete the science-experiment look?"

The nurse said, "Sorry," and rearranged my lovely hospital gown, which was now crawling with wires and tubes. She raised the head of my bed and propped me up on pillows. She tucked me under the covers and showed me the button to push for the TV and the one to push if I needed her.

Then I had to pee.

The nurse had to undo everything she'd just done, explaining which things plugged where. I pretended to listen.

"It seems like a lot now," she said, "but you'll get the hang of it."

I knew I wouldn't. We pushed aside the curtain. The bed next to mine was empty, but messy, so someone must live there. My roommate had the window side, and I was jealous. The streetlights were on. I looked down on the rooftop of the Blockbuster, and the dusty tops of a few scraggly palm trees. I could see the marquee for the Vista Theater. It seemed strange that there was still a world outside, going about its business.

I dragged my bomb into the bathroom and was about to close the door when the nurse stopped me. She wrote my name on a white plastic bowl and hooked it inside the toilet. "We need to measure everything that goes in, and everything that comes out," she said.

I made a face at her, but she smiled and said, "Call me when you're finished."

I closed the door and was finally alone. Just me. Well, me and my bowl, and my bomb. And my cancer.

{ THREE }

i hadn't noticed my aunt was gone, until she returned with a pile of notebooks and about six pens. Among the pile were sketchpads and drawing pens, which I put in the reject pile.

"Is this a self-esteem issue?" she asked, only half kidding. "Because you really are a good enough artist to draw with quality supplies."

"Gimme a break," I said. And thanked her for the blue Paper Mate and the college-ruled, three-subject spiral notebook. "These are exactly right," I said. "Perfect!"

The first thing I drew was my bomb. I'm no great artist, and that's a fact, not modesty. I'm a doodler. I don't squint and measure or erase and try to get things right—I just draw. It's more like humming than singing. Much more like dancing around the house than dancing onstage. Maybe it's more like sucking my thumb than anything else.

Anyway, I drew my bomb and the tangle of tubes and pipes and buttons and poles. In no time, the page became satisfyingly soggy and limp with ink. The side of my hand was blue, and so was the gauze on my wrist.

Nurses came in and out and made comments on my drawing. I tuned them out the best I could. One nurse with rubber duckies all over her nurse-shirt asked if she could have the picture when I was through, but I didn't get pissed—I figured she just didn't know any better.

Kay would be proud. She was the one who taught me that ages ago, when some kid in class bent over my desk to get a closer look at my soul—then told me I was "certifiably whacked." I'd told him where he could shove his opinion. But then Kay said *I* was the one who was out of line!

"People think drawing is a communication thing," she'd said. "A conversation, not a secret."

"Well, writing's like that, too," I'd answered, "but no one would lean over and read your journal and make comments! Or ask you to tear a page out and give it to them."

"But drawing *shows*," Kay explained. "Plus, everyone, myself included, is insanely jealous of how easy you make it look."

"Well, everyone, yourself included, is a jerk-wad," I grumbled.

"Which is why you've got to be patient with us," Kay said.

my dad was going home to explain things to my brother and feed Pupkin.

"Take Mom," I said.

But Mom shook her head and said, "I'll leave when *you* leave."

Dad kept going out in the hall, then coming back in, jingling his keys and the change in his pocket. "It's okay, Daddy," I said. "You can go." And, finally, he did.

My aunt left, too, after shaking her finger at my mom and warning her to *behave.*

I called Kay and she started to cry on the phone. "Just promise you won't die," she said.

"Cut it out," I said. "No one said anything about dying."

"Promise me," Kay said. "It's important."

"God, Kay," I said. "This wasn't *my* idea. And you're giving me the creeps."

"Shut up and promise!" she said.

I said, "All right, all right, I promise."

"I hate you," Kay mumbled.

I said, "I know."

"I'll be over there in the morning," she said.

"It so happens, I've got big biopsy plans for the morning," I told her. "I thought it might be fun to have one in my neck and one in each hip."

"What?" Kay shrieked.

"Don't ask," I answered. "I'm just telling you what they told me."

"Well, I'll be there," she said. "Where are you, anyway?"

"Children's."

"Aw, that's cute," Kay said. "But where's that?"

"Beats me. Somewhere in Hollywood, maybe Silver Lake. Near the Vista, where we saw that fifty-hour-long Chinese movie?"

Kay said, "My mom'll find it."

We were about to hang up, when I said, "Hey, Kay, do you have the school directory thing with everyone's phone number?"

She said, "Yeah, why?" But then she answered her own question. "Let me guess, you want to call *Jar-red.*"

I said, "I don't know, maybe."

"That's sick."

"Perfect!" I said. "I'm sick, it's sick—"

Kay said, "Jeez, Izz-a-smell"—her age-old name for me—"I can't believe you." But I heard her rummaging through the stuff on her desk, until she said, "Okay, but maybe think about it for a half a second first?"

"Just give me his number," I said.

So she did.

i dialed immediately, before I could chicken out.

A girl answered. His mom? Sister? Does he have a sister? I said, "Hi, is Jared there?"

And the girl grunted, "Just a sec."

Then Jared, sounding bored or half-asleep, said, "Hey."

Now what? "Jared?" I asked.

And he said, "Yeah."

I said, "Hi. This is Isabelle, from History?"

He said, "Hey," again, in a not particularly excited but not particularly disgusted, nothing sort of way. Then he waited for me to get to the point.

"I missed class today," I said.

He still waited. What did I expect? That he'd say *Yeah! I noticed and I've been worried sick all day*?

I said, "So . . ." but then I didn't know what to say. After about an hour and a half of agonizing mental illness, I said, "Was there any homework?"

Damn! Damn! Damn! Damn! That was so lame! I wanted to shoot myself for being such a wimp. I wanted to kick myself, throw myself out the window, run myself over with a truck and spit on my remains.

Jared said, "Homework?" as if he'd never heard of it. Then, "Nah, I don't think so. Want me to check?"

"No," I said. "Never mind."

And he waited again, to see if I had anything else to say or, in fact, any reason to exist.

I said, "Thanks," and "bye," and hung up.

While I was still burning, and blushing and scowling at the phone, it rang. My first thought was, Jared? Calling back?

But that was insane on every level.

It was Dad calling to say good night, and to tell me he'd looked up lymphoma on the Internet and everything was going to be fine.

"There's an eighty percent cure rate," he said. "And that takes into account children with other illnesses and risk factors, and kids who don't get decent medical care." He sounded reassured. "Eighty percent isn't half bad," he repeated.

I didn't ask what happened to the other 20 percent, the unluckier two out of every ten.

Dad put my brother on.

"You're faking, Lizard," Max said. "I know you are."

"Shhhh," I said. "Don't tell Daddy!"

my roommate skated in on her IV pole and introduced herself. I already knew her name was Carrie because I'd seen it scrawled on her pee-bowl in our bathroom. She was African American, with really long hair extensions that must've taken ages to braid.

She told me she'd been coming to Children's since she was four and knew all the tricks. She also said they try to room the teens together, although the girl who had my bed before me was only ten.

"She was leukemia," Carrie said. "Most kids on this floor are leukemia. Are you?"

I said, "No, they think I have lymphoma."

Carrie nodded. "I've seen a lot of that," she said. "But leukemia more."

I wanted to ask her about the lymphomas she'd seen, but that didn't seem polite.

"I usually get my transfusions in the day hospital," Carrie said. "But I come here lots of times when I get flare-ups. I'm a sickle-cell."

I guess I looked stupid.

"Sickle-cell anemia?" she asked.

"Oh."

"Where do you go to school?" she asked.

I told her, and asked where she went. Neither of us had ever heard of the other one's school. She said she was in seventh grade.

"Eighth," I said, surprised that I was older.

My mom leaned across my bed and asked Carrie if she was here all alone. I shot Mom a look. What if she *was*? Way to make her feel bad, Ma.

"No. My momma'll be in directly," Carrie said. "She's probably down in the chapel."

"They've got a chapel?" I asked. "Like a church kind of thing?"

"Now, where are you going to need to do more praying than a place like this?" Carrie asked. Then she noticed my drawing, and it was too late for me to slam my notebook shut or cover it or anything.

"Did you do that?" Carrie asked.

I didn't roll my eyes. I said, "Yeah."

"Wow," she said. "You're good. I can't draw a straight line."

I let that go, and did not ask what straight lines had to do with anything.

"Will you draw me?" she asked.

I said, "Nah, I'm no good at stuff like that."

"Aw, come on," she said. "Try!"

I *really* didn't want to. First of all, I suck at making people look like themselves, and second, I hate taking requests, and third, I just didn't want to.

"Pleeeeease?" she begged.

Normally I'd flip off anyone who nagged like that. But the fact that she was sitting on the edge of her hospital bed with an IV stuck in her arm somehow changed everything. I told her to strike a sexy pose, and she did— leaning sideways, legs crossed, head on her shoulder, eyelids at half mast.

I gave it my best shot.

Then I tore it out of my notebook and handed it over. Carrie looked at it closely for longer than it took me to draw it, but she gave no hint of an opinion. I started doodling something else so I wouldn't keep watching for her reaction. Here I was, in a hospital, punctured in several places, wired to a bomb, and attached to the wall, and I was worried about what some seventh-grade total stranger thought of a picture I'd drawn? Well, actually, yeah.

"Will you sign it?" Carrie asked.

That was a little embarrassing too, but I said sure and signed the damn thing.

Carrie put it on her bedside table. Then she crawled under her covers, turned her TV on, and fell instantly asleep.

Meanwhile, Mom wrestled a chair-bed open next to me, and tried to get comfortable. She hates TV, but tough. Carrie was the patient, not Mom.

i can't sleep with the TV blaring, either, but I probably wouldn't have slept anyway because every time I moved, my heart monitor got pissed and started to beep. Nurses had to come in every five seconds to un-beep me.

I gave up on sleep and drew the *Hazardous Waste Materials* mailbox slot, with a variety of slithery things escaping from it. That's how drawing works for me—I start with one idea, but then things happen to it; a line looks like a snake, so I chase it and it leads to something else. It's hard to explain, because I have no more clue how things'll end than anyone else does, but it sure passes the time.

A woman who must have been Carrie's mom came in, whispered *hi* and went to sleep in the chair beside Carrie.

I turned the page and drew the other box on the wall for contaminated needles. How had I missed *that* earlier? Then a whole bunch of tiny elflike men were squeezing out of the slot, lugging the dirty needles off with them, for some evil purpose, no doubt. I got so caught up in drawing that I completely forgot where I was, and why. But they don't let you forget for long. Nurses were always coming in to mess with my tubes or take my temperature or blood pressure or whatever.

They did the same things to Carrie, but she slept right through, with her TV jabbering away. I watched her shows awhile, and wondered if I was allowed to ask a nurse to turn down the volume.

Carrie and I had left the curtain open between us, but every single nurse tried to close it when they came in. By the time I got them trained to leave it open, the shift changed and a whole new crew started popping up at my bedside.

They each asked me how I felt.

Fine. I felt perfectly fine except for the pain in my wrist from the IV.

They all asked me if I had trouble breathing.

Finally, I asked one of them why everyone kept asking me that. "Don't you read each other's notes?" I asked.

And she said, "We have to make sure that the mass in your chest isn't restricting your lungs. And we don't know how fast it's growing, so we have to keep checking."

Mom gasped. Her face was a mask of horror.

Remind me never to ask anyone anything else the rest of my life. A *mass*? In my *chest*? Growing fast enough to suddenly squash my *lungs*?

Of course, as soon as I heard that, I couldn't breathe.

Mom tried to comfort me by saying the nurse was probably exaggerating or had me confused with some other patient.

I told my mom it was okay. I was fine. Then I lay still and stared at the ceiling till dawn.

people start banging things, wheeling squeaky carts, and making all kinds of noise around six am. A guy who looked vaguely familiar from yesterday came in and reminded me that he was my anesthesiologist. He asked my mom if I was allergic to any medications.

She teared up for her first time of the day. "Until now, Isabelle has been perfectly healthy," she said with a sigh.

"Let's just answer the questions, Mom," I said.

"The only medications she's ever taken were maybe for cramps or an ear infection," Mom said. "And she had no problem with them."

The man asked her if I'd eaten anything since midnight last night. Mom was stumped. She blinked at me, with her new blank look of confusion.

"No," I said. "I haven't eaten in ages." I didn't add that I was starving. This guy didn't look like he'd care.

I asked him if he was going to give me a shot.

He said, "No. You'll get everything through your IV." All three of us looked up at the bag of liquid dripping into my wrist. "And you'll be feeling no pain." He grinned. "We begin with Ativan, to relax you." His grin got bigger. I wondered if he wasn't on a bit of *Ativan* himself.

Meanwhile, I'd had to go to the bathroom the whole time the anesthesiologist guy was there, so the second he left, I hissed, "Mom! Help me unplug this stuff! Hurry!"

She scampered over but we couldn't puzzle out all the twisting cables. It was so confusing, we both suddenly got the giggles.

"No! Don't make me pee!" I gasped, trying not to laugh and trying not to wake Carrie.

Mom grabbed a plug. "Let's try this."

"No!" I giggled. "If we pull the wrong thing, my head'll fall off."

"Buzz the nurse." Mom hiccupped between laugh attacks. "She *said* to call if we needed anything."

I don't know why that made me crack up even harder. I had to double over and clamp my legs together. "She meant . . . she meant if we needed anything *medical!*" I sputtered. "Crutches or . . bandages or something."

Mom snickered back at me as if crutches were a hoot. Her tears were the uncontrollable-laugh kind this time.

We must've woken Carrie. *Snip, snap,* she had me and my bomb free and on our way, laughing and leaking, to the bathroom. I heard Mom's tee-hees simmering down behind me, with the occasional snort.

Then I saw the bowl with my name on it, and decided, no, not this time. It hadn't sounded right yesterday, when my pee landed in that dry bowl. And it felt wrong not to flush. My parents were always ragging on my brother about that.

I felt so sneaky, letting my pee splash where it belonged. Then I flushed, bye-bye!

carrie wasn't one of those groggy morning types. She went from zero to sixty in two seconds flat. Chattering away, bouncing around. "Who's on this morning?" she asked me. "Shelly?"

I didn't know if she meant the TV or the nursing staff or what. So I just shrugged.

"I'm going to order breakfast," she said. "Did you eat already?"

I told her I was going for a biopsy and couldn't eat.

She slammed down the phone. "I'll wait till you're gone then," she said. "It would be mean to chow down right in front of you. What are you getting checked?"

"My neck?" I said. "And my hips?"

She nodded. "The hip thing is a bone marrow," she said. "I've had that."

"Does it hurt?" I asked.

"Well, yeah." Carrie shrugged. "But you know, later."

I didn't know. Bone marrow sounded deep. Wasn't the marrow way in the middle of the bone? My hips started to ache in anticipation. I looked over at my mom and I could see my hip pain written all over her face. It was that *Picture of Dorian Gray* thing again.

Then a guy showed up with a wheelchair and said he was there to escort me to a CAT scan. I almost made a crack about kitty cats, but I bet he'd heard that before, a couple hundred times.

My teeth felt crummy and I needed a shower, but he made it clear that I was supposed to get in his wheelchair now.

"I don't need a ride," I said. "I can walk."

But he said it was hospital policy or something. And my mom didn't want me making trouble. I'd never ridden in a wheelchair before. It didn't remind me of anything.

We turned down a hall labeled *Nuclear Radiology*, which sounded awfully serious. My driver parked me next to a wall, sort of at an angle. He told an Indian woman with a bindi dot on her forehead that I was there for a CAT scan, and then he left, saying nothing to me. Suddenly I felt like a *thing*, a nonperson that he'd delivered like a load of mail—or garbage.

A few minutes later, the Indian woman came back and wheeled me into a cold little room with a big, ugly, beige torture device in the center.

She made me lie down on the machine, with my arms over my head, then she taped my feet together, rattling on that I had to keep still and follow the directions when I heard them, to hold and release my breath.

She told me the scan would be noisy and she showed me a button to push if I couldn't stand it. She said the test would take about twenty minutes.

A different woman appeared to inject radioactive dye through my IV.

"Hey!" I said. "That shit could give me *cancer!*"

"Izzy, please!" Mom said. "Watch your language."

It was a lame joke anyway.

"This might feel a little warm," the injection lady said. And the split second the words were out of her mouth, my face started to burn weirdly, and my mouth tasted like tinfoil.

An older guy in blue tried to move Mom behind the protective wall, but she wouldn't stay there. He gave up and handed her a lead apron to wear.

This new tic of hers, that she couldn't be more than six and a half inches from me, was a little much. Not that I'd rather do any of it alone, but imagine how touching and romantic all this could've been if it were, say, *Jared* glommed onto me. He by my side; our eyes locked. My brave smile, his slavish devotion and unbelievable studly blue-eyed hotness . . .

Someone pushed a button or something and I slid headfirst into a ringlike thing. The roar began, but was broken up by a woman's bossy voice ordering me to stay still and telling me when to breathe.

Insert girl. Radiate. Deafen. Remove.

When they rolled me out, the first thing I saw was Mom, crying. The technician asked her if she was all right, and Mom looked at him like he was crazy. "How could I be all right?" she asked.

"Mom! Get a grip!" I said. "He works with this all the time. Do you have to be the looniest mom here?"

Mom turned her befuddled face to me. "Huh?"

"Cope," I said.

Mom nodded.

The tech helped me off the table and back into my wheelchair. "It's hard on the moms," he told me with a wink. "You have to be patient."

"No, I don't!" I said with more force than I'd intended. "*I* have cancer. *Me.* Not her."

Mom winced at the word *cancer.* "Call it *lymphoma*," she said. "It sounds better."

I rolled my eyes, and the technician laughed. His front tooth was gold, and for a split second, I hoped he was a pirate who'd kidnap me and hold me for ransom, far away, on his creaky old ship.

But no such luck.

{ FOUR }

dad was pacing the hall by the elevators when we got back to my floor. Mom really let her sobs rip at the sight of him. "Izzy has been so brave!" Mom cried. "She's been an incredible trouper."

"Like I have a choice?"

"You're amazing!" Mom cried harder.

People in the hall turned to look. They, too, were on the blood-cancer floor. No doubt they also had a few things to worry about, but you didn't hear *them* wailing in the hall.

"Dad! Would you shut her up, please?"

"Don't be mean to your mother," Dad said. "This is hard for her."

"It's all right," Mom said. "She doesn't mean anything by it. She has a lot on her mind."

You think?

I hated it when they called me *she* and talked about me like I wasn't there. Add that to my long *things I hate* list. A list that was getting longer by the minute.

When we got to my room, I asked Carrie if there was a cafeteria or something.

"Down on B," she said. "Tiger elevators."

I turned to my parents, "Why don't you go get a cup of coffee or breakfast or whatever?" I said.

They shook their heads no. "They could come for you for the biopsy any time now!" Mom explained.

"And they can't do it without you?" I asked. "Are you handing them the scalpel?"

My parents just peered at me with the kind of dim, unfocused eyes you see in nature flicks of newborn and newly hatched things. They were hopeless, so I asked Carrie if she wanted to show me how to ride my IV.

"Sure," she said, and hopped out of bed. "Just stand on it with one foot, and push off with the other."

It was easy.

"Izzy-pie, be careful!" Dad called after me.

"how was your scan?" Carrie asked as we coasted down the hall.

"Compared to what?" I asked back. "Could've been worse, I suppose, but they could do a lot to make that stuff better."

Carrie said, "Better?"

"Yeah. Make the machine more like a carnival ride or something. Paint teeth all around the ring and pipe in the sounds of a monster chewing, going, 'Yum! You're delicious!'" I said. "Or you know that voice that tells you to breathe? Why couldn't they use Daffy Duck for that? Or have someone cracking jokes, or making fart noises?"

Carrie laughed.

"I mean, they paint the lobby bright colors, why not *really* make it a kids' hospital?"

Carrie introduced me to practically everyone on the floor. Most of the kids were much younger. We skipped the rooms that were still dark, and the ones that had crowds around the beds, and the ones with cribs.

In one room, she said, "This is Marilee. She's a sickle-cell, too. This is Izzy. She's an artist." I laughed, thinking Carrie had compared having sickle-cell to being an artist, but she hadn't meant it that way.

Marilee said hi. I said hi back.

A bag of deep reddish brown liquid was dripping down a tube, into Marilee, from a pole like our IV poles. When I realized it was blood, I felt a shiver shoot down my legs. I hoped I didn't look as freaked as I felt.

Then we came to a set of double doors with a sign that said, *Transplant Area.* That gave me a different shiver. It had never occurred to me that anything as serious as *transplant*s went on so close to where I lived my regular life. So close to the Vista Theater.

As we neared the nurses' station, Carrie told me that people were always bringing cookies and treats to the staff, but you had to get there fast or they'd be gone. Then she covered her mouth. "Oops! I forgot you're not allowed to eat!"

We stopped at what Carrie called the "playroom." It was full of sunlight and windows. Little arts-and-crafts tables were set up, with tiny plastic chairs and colorful pillows on the floor. A tall, not bad-looking guy about my age was looking through a shelf of old videos. He wasn't in a hospital gown or pajamas, but he wore the same bracelet as me and had slippers on.

Carrie said, "Hi, Sam!"

He looked around, tossing floppy dark bangs out of his eyes, and said, "Hi."

"This is Izzy. She's new."

He said, "Hi" again, and held up two tapes. "I'm torn between *Beauty and the Beast* and *The Muppet Movie*. What do you think?"

"*Muppets*," I said.

"I've seen it about forty times, though," he answered.

"Well, *Beauty and the Beast* then," I laughed.

"At least fifty," he said. "Probably more like sixty."

I rode my IV over to the shelf. There were a lot of Care Bears and Disney and Wee Sing. "I loved this one," I said, and handed him *Wee Sing in Sillyville.*

He held it to his chest and said, "Thanks." Then he pointed at a stack of board games and asked Carrie and me if we'd like to play a rousing round of Candy Land.

"I'd like to," I said, "but I think I have a biopsy now-ish." Then I added, "Maybe later?"

"You girls and your biopsies," he said.

When Carrie and I skated out, she said, "You like him, I can tell."

I shrugged.

"He's a leukemia," she said.

When we got back to our room, Carrie's mom was there, wrapped in a bathrobe, with a towel on her head, and introduced herself.

She told my mom where the showers were and other things about life here. While the moms talked, Dad paced. This time I went to the bathroom *before* getting reattached to the wall.

And when I came out, Kay was there! I tried to run to her, but my bomb wouldn't let me. So I just said, "It's about time you dragged your lazy butt in here."

"Hi, Izz!" Kay said, smiling the kind of smile you'd smile if a guy had a gun in your back and told you to act normal. Her mom was grinning her head off, too. "Great room!" Kay added.

"It is! So bright and cheerful!" Kay's mom agreed, showing me all her teeth.

I looked behind me to see if I was being followed by some monster. I looked down to see if my gown was covering everything it should. I checked for embarrassing stains, toilet paper stuck to my foot. I still didn't get it, so I asked, "What's wrong with you two?"

"Not a thing!" Kay's mom said, smiling even bigger. "You look great, Isabelle, really."

"Oh," I said finally. "It's the *cancer*."

"*Lymphoma*," Mom corrected.

I wound my way to my bed. I could feel everyone watching me. "Carrie, this is my best friend, Kay," I said. "She's not always so weird."

Carrie said, "Hello."

Kay grinned extra insanely and said, "Hi, Carrie! Nice to meet you!"

That was my mom's cue to burst into tears. Kay's mom gave a little squeak of surprise, then bustled Mom out into the hall.

I leaned over and poked Kay in the chest. "What have you done with my friend Kay?"

Kay let out a giant breath and turned back into herself. She crawled into bed next to me. "My mom said to act cheerful," she explained. "She said it's sort of the law in hospitals."

We played with the bed controls until we had our knees bent up almost to our heads. I told Kay there was a cute guy here with leukemia.

"He liked you," Carrie said.

I went, "*Pfttt*."

"Well, he never asked *me* to play Candy Land," she said. Then all three of us cracked up over how bizarre that sounded.

A nurse came in to say they'd be taking me to my biopsy soon. She didn't seem surprised by the sight of me and Kay folded practically in half. She just pushed buttons on my bomb and messed with my IV.

When she left, we flattened the bed a little and asked Carrie if she wanted to come over. Carrie was there in a blink with a deck of cards. But as soon as we had the hands dealt for hearts, an orderly appeared to take me down to surgery.

Kay's mom followed him into the room. "Come along, Kay," she said through her grin. "It's time to go."

"You can go if you want, but I'm staying here to wait for Izz-a-smell," Kay announced.

Her mom's voice got higher and her smile got wider. "No, honey. You have to get to school! We promised your father. Maybe I can bring you back later, or tomorrow. When are visiting hours?" she asked my mom.

But Mom was beyond speech. She clutched the back of the wheelchair as if it were a life raft. Dad stood beside her, looking grim.

"Mom, pleeeeeease?" Kay begged.

Their back-and-forth continued as I was rolled away. "Anyone want to bet on who wins?" I asked my parents, but they were both too freaked to speak.

Hey, weren't they supposed to be trying to cheer *me* up, instead of the other way around?

I'd never had an operation before. I didn't think it sounded a bit fun. "Let me get this straight," I said. "If we already know I have cancer—"

"*Lymphoma*," Mom said, under her breath.

"Then what are these biopsies for?"

Dad answered, "To see what kind it is. Different lymphomas respond to different treatments. Didn't you hear the explanation your oncologist gave?"

Give me a break. How was I supposed to remember which of those people was my oncologist? Less than twenty-four hours ago, I didn't even know what an oncologist was, and I'd never *heard* of lymphoma.

"Don't let them put in that PICC line thing, or port or whatever they call it," I said. "I'm totally serious. I do *not* want it."

My parents both looked so scared that I couldn't tell if they heard me.

"No PICC line!" I repeated.

Three women in hospital scrubs came in smiling and took me from the guy who'd wheeled me down. One woman had me move from the wheelchair to a rolling bed with sides like a crib. Another one hugged my mom and told her they'd take good care of me. Mom, of course, was crying. The third fiddled around with my IV and told me she was adding "happy juice."

"I really don't want a PICC line," I said to one of the ladies. "I mean, I don't particularly want cancer, either, but I especially don't want a PICC line."

The woman heard me. "I'll get your surgeon," she said. And she did.

A few minutes later, a red-faced, short-haired woman I dimly recognized from yesterday's blur of faces appeared. "I hear you're refusing the PICC line," she said. "I think that's an unreasonable stand."

I shrugged.

"It's considerably easier to put it in now, while you're under anesthesia. We can always remove it if you don't need it. Otherwise, you may have to undergo a second surgery, later. Or possibly have it inserted while you're awake."

"Well, I don't want it," I insisted. I knew I sounded like a brat, but the idea of that thing was more than I could stand.

Then the world went soft and fuzzy. One of the nurses wearing a shower cap told me that I was feeling the Ativan. I passed out, thinking that *Ativan* was a lovely, lovely word.

I woke up barfing. Mom was wiping my face. Dad held a bowl under my chin. One of the doctors or nurses or someone was saying that I was allergic to morphine. I pried open my eyes to see who was talking and there was my brother.

"Hey, Lizard," Max said, looking scared.

I looked around to see what he was afraid of. There was a mob of people around my bed.

Great. I had puke in my hair and probably stunk to high heaven. I closed my eyes to make them disappear, but then I forced them open again to check. Okay, at least none of them seemed to be Jared.

When I woke next, it was just my parents. "Did they put in the PICC?" I asked. But I guess it came out funny, because neither of them seemed to know what I'd asked.

Then it was dark, the curtain was closed, Carrie's TV was loud, and my mom was mashed up in the chair beside my bed, snoring. She looked kind of cute.

I'd been bullying her lately. I knew this whole can-cer, hospital thing was a nightmare for her, and I told myself not to be so mean. How hard could it be to just be a little more patient with her looniness? She couldn't help how annoying she was.

I got up to go to the bathroom, started unplugging things, and that's the last thing I remember—until I came to, surrounded by nurses.

"You fainted," Mom explained, looking guilty as sin. "I must've been asleep."

I wanted to tell her not to sweat it, but I didn't have the strength.

I woke again and was starving. It had been ages since I'd eaten, except through my wrist. The room was light. My mom wasn't on her chair. Where was she?

I called, "Mom?"

Carrie answered, "Sleeping Beauty wakes!" She pulled back our curtains and sunshine flooded the room. I saw, too, that half the downstairs gift shop had moved up here. It seemed I was now the proud owner of a fairy princess figurine and a crap load of stuffed animals and balloons.

"What's a girl got to do to get food around here?" I asked, wondering where my mom was.

Carrie flew over to my bed with a menu and said, "Call room service!" So I did.

Finally, my parents crept into the room. Mom pushed my hair off my forehead and asked how I felt. Dad patted my knee and looked stunned.

"Who won?" I asked.

They blinked at me.

"Kay or her mom?"

Still no comprehension.

"Was Kay still here when I got back from the biopsy or did she come back later?"

Mom furrowed her forehead in concentration.

Dad just patted my knee again.

My food came and I ate like a pig. Mom told me to take it easy, but I ignored her. My right hand was still taped to that board, and it wasn't easy to eat as a lefty, but I did my very best. Pudding, cheeseburger, fries, corn, cookies, chocolate milk. At last, I sat back like a boa constrictor digesting a caribou. *Ahhhh!*

Everyone was looking at me.

I belched and said, "What?"

"We got your biopsy results," my dad said. "And we're glad to report that the kind of lymphoma you have is called Hodgkin's. They're going to start chemotherapy today."

I didn't know what to ask, so I didn't ask anything. Both my parents looked totally trashed. If they *had* to look like that, I wished they'd do it somewhere else. That reminded me of Kay's mom's theory of *hospital smiles* and I practically agreed with her.

My dad, who takes great comfort from numbers, started spouting statistics. "They have an eighty-six percent cure rate with Hodgkin's. And seventy percent of those are put in remission by the first round of chemo. And *wagga* percent of cases are *wagga wagga* by eight rounds of chemo, two weeks apart—"

I interrupted, "What *is* chemotherapy?"

Mom blinked.

"It's chemicals, medicines," Dad said. "That kill the cancer. I don't know *exactly*."

"Pills?" I asked.

"No. I'm pretty sure they inject it," Dad said. "Through your IV, I guess."

"Where's Kay?" I asked.

My parents looked at each other as if that was not the question they were prepared for. I grabbed the phone. Kay answered on the first ring.

"Come!" I demanded.

"I can't!" Kay wailed back. "My parents won't let me."

"Tell them I have *cancer!*" I said.

"I swear, they won't. Mostly, my dad."

"Why the hell not?"

Kay missed a beat, then said, "I sort of lost it last night, when you were acting all weird."

"What did I do?"

"Well, threw up all over yourself, passed out, and your eyes rolled up in your head. Very *Exorcist*."

"Eeew."

"Right. So I flipped a little, and now my dad says it's too much for me. Plus, he says I can't miss any more school."

I'd always hated Kay's bossy, overprotective father, but I didn't say so. Instead, I said, "You missed what? A day? One stinking day of eighth grade? Like that's such a big deal?"

"Tell me about it," Kay said.

I half-remembered the crowd around my bed. "Who was here?" I asked.

Kay knew what I meant. "Jared wasn't," she said.

Phew! That was a relief. "Does he know?" I asked.

"Everyone knows," Kay said. "Didn't you see the package of letters?"

I looked around. "Mom? Do I have a package of letters here somewhere?"

Mom looked confused.

"Over on the table," Carrie said, pointing.

Dad got it for me. My name was written on the front of the envelope, with a bunch of hearts and stickers. I turned it over and dumped the notes on my lap. There were a lot. I opened the first one and started reading it to Kay.

"'Dear Isabelle,'" it said, "'I am so sad about you being sick. I thought about you all night long! I will always remember your smile and what a great artist you were, and funny! Love xo Samantha.'"

"Eat shit, Samantha," I said.

"Izzy!" my mother gasped.

"Well, it's like she's writing to a dead person. Isn't that what she means by 'remembering' my smile? Please. She's got me smiling down from heaven as her own personal angel. Makes me want to puke."

"And we all know how good you are at that!" Kay said.

"Why don't they just write, *Dear Cancer, Thank you for being in Izzy's body instead of mine!*" I asked.

Mom shook her head and gave me her disapproving look.

I opened the next card. "'Dear Izzy, Get well soon and hurry back! Miss you to bits! Love and kisses forever, Alison.'

"Who the hell's Alison?" I asked.

Kay laughed in one ear and Carrie in the other. My dad smiled, a little.

"I think it's very sweet," Mom said. "Must you scorn *everything*?"

"Here ya go," I said, handing Mom the pile. "Have fun."

"Kay? Did he write one or not?"

Kay knew who I meant. "Not," she answered. "But I bet there'll be another whole batch tomorrow."

I wanted to hang up. What good was having cancer and being in the hospital if it didn't even make Jared write me a love letter? Or a crummy get-well card, at least.

"Tell your parents that if I die in here, it'll be their fault," I told Kay.

"Izz! What a thing to say!" Mom gasped.

"You don't like it, don't listen to my phone calls," I said, and stuck my tongue out at her.

Mom rolled her eyes.

"I'll do my best," Kay said. "Maybe a hunger strike will work."

"No, that's too slow," I whined. "I want you here now!"

"I know," Kay said. "Me, too." And we hung up.

Mom said, "Here's a sweet one," and she started reading: "'Dearest Isabelle, We are all praying for you. You are in our thoughts always and we know you will triumph over this!'"

"Who's that?"

"It's signed, 'Ms. Lyons,'" Mom said.

"She gave me a D in PE last year," I said. "Remember?"

Mom ignored me and started reading the next one "'Dear Izzy . . .'"

I just wished everyone would leave. Better yet, they could stay here, enjoying the letters and being glad it's Hodgkin's instead of who-knows-what—and I'd leave.

{ FIVE }

i looked like shit in the bathroom mirror, but there wasn't a thing I could do about it. My hair was filthy, but I didn't even have a hair tie to pull it back. There was a bandage on my neck, smudged with blood. I wondered if I'd have a scar. Would I have to wear turtlenecks to cover it, even in ninety-eight-degree summer?

There was a knock on the door. "Helloooo? Isabelle? Are we all right in there?" It was an unfamiliar voice talking baby talk. I hate baby talk.

"Just a minute," I said, and flushed the toilet to make it sound real. Then I remembered that I was no longer among the flushers. If this were the plot of a murder mystery, I thought, the flushing or not flushing could be a clue that only those who'd had to save their pee would get.

The woman waiting for me was in regular clothes, so I knew she wasn't a nurse. "Isabelle!" she said, "I'm so, *so* happy to meet you." She stuck out her hand for me to shake. I gave her my taped and boarded-up hand but she didn't laugh. She sort of pinched my fingertips in a prissy shake instead.

"I'm Pamela Ann Carter," she said, still in baby talk, although now she'd seen me and knew I wasn't four. "I'm one of the psychiatric social workers here at Children's Hospital Los Angeles!" In case I didn't know where I was. "And I just wanted to check in and see how you're getting along."

"Shitty," I said, creeping back to my bed. "They knocked me out, and slit my throat. They drilled holes in both my hips, and I puked on myself in front of everyone."

My mom opened her mouth to correct me, but I squelched her with a look.

Ms. Whatever-Her-Name-Was turned to my mom "Hostility and sarcasm are to be expected from our teens at a time like this," she explained helpfully.

I grabbed my pen and notebook, inspired to do this smarmy woman's portrait. I bet she thought she was hot shit. I practically cackled as I gave her tights and a billowing superhero cape. Then I added a halo because her friends, if she had any, probably thought she was a friggin' saint for working with cancer kids. Saint Shit. I emblazoned *S.S.* in a crest on her chest, and snickered.

I glanced up from my drawing when a big, tall black woman came in wearing a huge blue rubber apron, with a mask dangling around her neck. She looked like a giant Smurf.

"Isabelle Miller?" she asked, looking from me to Carrie.

I pointed at Carrie and went back to my sketch.

"She's just kidding," St. Shit tattled, patting my bed. "*This* is Isabelle, our little joker."

"I'm here to give you your chemo," the Smurf said to me, snapping on a pair of blue latex gloves. "My name is Tanya."

"I'll come back later then," S.S. baby-talked. "And we can get to know each other better. Would you like that, Isabelle?"

I said, "No."

"Izzy!" Mom sputtered. "Don't be rude!"

So I smiled sweetly, and said, "Sorry, I meant no, *thank you.*"

My mom followed the twit into the hall, probably to apologize for me. I think Mom was afraid that if I ticked off anyone here, they'd take medical revenge.

The Smurf closed the curtain between me and Carrie, then began laying a bunch of truly horrifying vials and tubes and bandages on my table. She also had a metal box that looked like a safe. She took secret objects out of there and covered them with a towel.

"Must be pretty bad, if it's even worse than the rest of these weapons," I said.

The Smurf nodded. "Some kids don't want to see all this," she said. "And I don't blame them. The question is, how much do *you* want to know?"

That was an interesting question. I thought about it. The Smurf didn't rush me for an answer; she was opening little packets and arranging things.

"I guess I should want to know everything," I said. "Right?"

"There're no *should*s with this," she answered.

"Okay, well, is it going to hurt?" I asked.

And she said, "It could. But it's different with everyone, so there's no telling. You're getting four different drugs." She named them, but the names just sounded like gibberish. "ABVD for short."

"Most people do fine with three of them," she said. "But the fourth can sting going in. That's why I'm wearing this getup—so if it spills on me, I won't get burned."

"And you're putting that in my veins?" I asked.

She nodded seriously. No baby talk, no making it light. She was scaring the hell out of me, but I trusted her.

I asked her if this was the kind of chemo that would make my hair fall out, and she said, "Yes, probably, although everyone responds differently."

"What's your name again?" I asked.

"Tanya White."

Tanya did things to my IV and said she was giving me Zofran to prevent the nausea that the chemo can cause. "You'll have it in pill form, later," she said.

"I can't swallow pills," I said.

She squinted at me and said, "Big girl like you?"

I nodded.

"No matter," she said. "You can always chew them up, or crush them in peanut butter. But for now, the first thing we've got to do is find a good vein," she said.

"Good luck," I said, showing her my bruised and battered arms.

She nodded and started examining me. "I thought I saw you sketching when I came in," she said. "Do you draw right- or left-handed?"

"Right."

Tanya dropped my right arm and said, "No point in messing with your talent hand." She picked a vein on the inside of my left forearm, and slapped it. She got the needle in on the first poke. I was impressed. Terrified, but impressed. Mom looked at Tanya as if she were our savior, and maybe she was.

"Do you know why chemotherapy makes your hair fall out?" she asked me.

I said no.

"Would you like to know?"

"I guess."

"Because it kills fast-growing cells. Cancer cells are fast-growing, but so are your hair cells, and white blood cells. White blood cells fight infection, so after we kill off a bunch of them, like we're about to, you'll have to be extra careful. Wash your hands like a fanatic. Don't hang around sick folk."

She was taping the syringe to my arm as she talked. "The inside of your mouth is made of cells that divide rapidly as well," she said. "That's why your mouth heals quickly when you burn it on cocoa. But that's also why you might develop sores in your mouth."

"Fabulous," I said. "So much to look forward to." Then I asked, "So if the chemo kills my hair, will that mean it's also killing the cancer?"

"The two things aren't necessarily related," Tanya said. "But it'll work. This stuff is smart and powerful and it'll kick the cancer's butt."

I ran my fingers through my hair. True, I'd complained about it endlessly, wanting Kay's shiny black hair, or my friend Penelope's bouncy blond-red curls. But now I touched my plain brown hair and felt a wave of grief.

"I love my hair," I said.

"It'll come back," Tanya said. "And lots of times, it comes back better."

I squinted at her to see if she was lying.

She squinted back at me. Then she raised her gloved hand and said, "Scout's honor."

My mom touched my hair, which I knew needed a shampoo, and said, "Izzy was blond as a baby." I saw one of her tears ping down on the sheet.

"This can take anywhere from an hour on up," Tanya said. "We'll have to see as we go." She held up a syringe. "First, I'm going to flush the line with this saline solution. It won't hurt."

She squirted the stuff through the needle in my arm.

This made no sense. How could this be me? It fit with nothing else in my life. The old *Sesame Street* song popped into my head, the one that showed four things, like a football, a tennis ball, a soccer ball, and a tiger, while they asked which one didn't belong.

This one would have three pictures of me and Kay at school or me and my family at home or camping on the beach last summer, or out for Thai food, or me picking my nose or fantasizing about Jared or drawing or some other normal thing—and the fourth picture would be me here, doing *this*.

Tanya brought a hugely exaggerated syringe out from under the towel. It was enormous, like what they'd have in a cartoon. And the liquid in it was bright red.

"You're kidding, right?" I asked.

Mom grabbed my shoulder.

"Easy does it," Tanya said, as she attached the gigantic syringe to the needle in my arm. "This one has to be pushed," she said. "The others, though, can drip through your IV."

"Pushed?"

"See?" She was slowly pressing the plunger on the monster syringe with her thumb, shooting the bright red chemo into me. It hurt.

"Your urine will be pink tomorrow," Tanya said. "Just thought I'd warn you."

Mom asked Tanya how she kept from getting depressed working there.

"I like to think I'm helping," Tanya said, as if it had never occurred to her to be glum.

Mom nearly killed herself apologizing.

Tanya cut her off to say, "Of course, it doesn't help that the kids are terrified of me and start crying when they see me coming. They call me the blue wall."

I laughed.

"One for me," Tanya said. "I count laughs and keep score. It's two to one right now."

"I scored two?" I asked.

"Yep," Tanya said without raising her eyes from her work. "One was when you tried to pass me off on your roommate. And two was when you told that Missy Social Worker where to get off."

I flicked my notebook open with my good hand and showed Tanya my *S.S.* drawing. She laughed, bumping my score to three.

I wondered how anyone could be terrified of such a nice blue wall. She was my favorite nurse so far.

Tanya fed the second chemo into a branch of my IV tube. It gave me a headache, but nothing I couldn't stand. The laugh score was six to three, my lead.

She said I could go ahead and draw or read or sleep or whatever and not to feel like I had to keep her company, so I called Kay, but her dad said she wasn't home. I thought of calling Jared, but Mom was sitting right there, and I'd probably just act like a moron again. That last call was bad enough, thank you.

So I doodled a few of Tanya's ghastly toys. I put the mammoth syringe on wheels like a Civil War cannon, chasing down a little bug that looked something like the kid across the hall. He was a tiny guy with such amazingly thick black eyelashes that I doubted he could hoist his eyelids up all the way.

Meanwhile, I wondered what it was like to be Tanya, and the rest of the people working on that strange space station of odd, beeping machines and red chemicals, surrounded by a constant parade of illness. Especially the upside-down lives of the folks on the night shift. Did they have a parallel society on the outside?

Then everything changed. I'd heard that if you get bitten by a black widow spider, you feel the path of the poison move through you with incredible agony. That was the fourth injection.

Tanya pushed a tiny bit on the syringe, and pain screamed through me as if she were injecting fire. I couldn't believe my arm *looked* the same from the outside.

"There's no rush," Tanya said. "We'll take it real slow. Your job is to tell me when you're ready for me to push a few more drops—and when you want me to stop."

Whenever I said *stop*, Tanya stopped. She never tried to sneak in an extra squirt to hurry things up, and she didn't start pushing again until I told her she could. But telling Tanya to start pushing was the hardest thing I'd ever done.

When I *couldn't* make myself say it anymore, Tanya would wait awhile, then say, "Ready to go on?"

I'd nod, although it wasn't really possible to be *ready*.

We took a break every now and then for her to flush the line and check to make sure the needle was still in the vein. She explained that if it slipped out into the tissue of my arm, I'd get burned.

I didn't know how that could've been any worse than now, which was as if a grenade had gone off inside me, or my arm was being gnawed off by a shark. There were no more laugh points scored on either side.

Finally, Tanya announced that the last drop of chemo was in. My mom collapsed in a heap as if she'd been holding her breath all these hours.

Tanya pulled out the needle, bandaged my arm, packed up her stuff, and left. Now I got why kids panicked when they saw her coming.

i must've fallen asleep, because next, I was awakened in the dark by the worst nausea of my life, times ten. The puking I'd done after the biopsy was nothing compared to this.

The nurses brought pills that fizzed on my tongue, and they put stuff in my IV and gave me a shot in my ass that I was too sick to even be afraid of. "Booty juice," the nurse called it, unless I dreamed that. But nothing helped.

Carrie came through the curtain and I remember her saying, "It's all in your head. Not in a *bad* way, but your body is yelling, *Help! I'm being poisoned!* And it tells your brain, *Quick! Get this nasty poison out of me!* Meaning the chemo. Your brain thinks you must've eaten something bad, so it's telling the rest of your body to get rid of it. The only way it knows how is to throw up."

I tried to understand what she was saying.

Then she said, "Anyway, it was nice knowing you. I'm going home."

I would've said good-bye or registered my surprise that she was leaving so suddenly, but a huge wave of vomit rushed up my throat and out. It came with such force it felt like it would blow my whole face off, rather than just blast though my mouth. My head throbbed, my ears rang. My teeth felt loose, and I itched as if I were crawling with bugs.

I'd had no idea a human could feel so totally awful and not die.

People came and went. Doctors, nurses, Kay, Aunt Lucy. Unless it was a dream, the cute boy, Sam, from the playroom even showed up, rattling the Candy Land box.

But I was busy—my life was centered on misery and there was no room for other thought.

I half-remember some nurse trying to clean me off. Changing my hospital gowns and sheets, then moments later coming back because I'd barfed all over everything again.

Later, there was a new girl in Carrie's bed. I stumbled past her on my way to the bathroom. Actually, I just assumed she was a girl, all I really saw was a lump of blankets in the dark. She and her family had the curtains closed and the lights off.

The new girl left her pee-bowl in the toilet, which I didn't appreciate. I had to touch it to put mine in. That made me hate whoever-she-was with as much energy as I could muster, which wasn't much.

At some point, I realized I was no longer attached to anything. Not even an IV. I heard my parents talking to someone about taking me home. But I was too dizzy and sick to care.

you don't just put your shoes on and walk out the door of a hospital. Hordes of people have to come and talk and talk and talk to you first. It seemed to me that Carrie told me she was leaving one second, and was gone the next—I don't know how she did it.

But finally, I was loaded into a wheelchair with a lap full of fairies and a pink puke pail stocked with medical supplies. They handed me pages of instructions and a bag of green-and-white striped surgical masks that I was told to wear whenever I was in public or near anyone sick or around construction or dust or mold, and when I came to the hospital.

They made me put one on right then. It felt sweaty and claustrophobic.

"I walked in here on my own two feet, feeling just ducky," I said to my dad, "and now look."

At last, I was wheeled to the door.

The outside smelled fabulously of smog, car exhaust, freedom!

I got carsick, though, within a few blocks of the hospital, and by the time we pulled up our driveway, I felt green and wobbly. I crept inside with the sofa in mind, but Kay was there, and my brother, and Aunt Lucy and a few neighbors. They all rushed me with hugs, and Pupkin went nuts, jumping and barking and thwacking everyone with his tail.

His bark seemed louder and more shrill; it hurt my ears. And what dumbass cranked the music so damn loud?

The overpowering smell of barbecue filled the air, and the sight of pies and brownies on the table was somehow nauseating. Max shoved a huge vase of flowers in my face and told me that Mom's office had sent them. Then he practically suffocated me with a bunch of Mylar balloons that Kay said were from school. The first thing I did was race to the bathroom to celebrate my homecoming with a big, noisy puke. After that, I slept for a day and a half.

{ SIX }

kay woke me with a shove. "Come on, Izz, get up. I'm sick of watching you sleep!"

"Excuse me, I have *cancer*, I can do whatever I want," I said.

"But I've got so much to tell you!"

"Yeah? Like what?"

"Well, let me see . . ."

I closed my eyes and snuggled back down in my blankets.

"For one thing, you ought to see Amanda," Kay said.

"Amanda who?"

"You know, that girl with the cheesy pink glasses? She was in our art class," Kay said. "Remember?"

My mom came into my room to ask Kay if she'd washed her hands.

Kay said yes.

Mom asked if she was sure.

"Positive," Kay said, holding them up to show her. But she offered to do it again if it would make my mother more comfortable.

Mom thought about it a second, then said, "No, that's okay," and left my room.

"That's her new thing," I explained. "She won't even let Pupkin sleep with me anymore."

"Tell me about it!" Kay said. "It's been a nonstop cleaning frenzy. When you were conked out, she had *me* scrubbing. Your caseworker told her that you don't have any defense against germs."

"I have a caseworker?" I asked. "Isn't that like a detective or something?"

"I'm telling you something, if you don't mind."

"What?"

"I'm worried about her."

"My caseworker?"

"No! Your mom!" Kay said. "I think she has totally flipped, cleanliness-wise. Haven't you noticed that the whole house reeks of bleach? You can smell it halfway down the block. If you ask me, bleach fumes are way worse for you than plain old dirt."

Kay plopped down on the foot of my bed. "Every time I call to say I'm coming over, your mom asks me if I'm sick, or if I've been near anyone who's ever been sick in their entire life. And she tells me to put on clean clothes before I come, in case I got germed out in the world without knowing it. And," Kay said, wiggling her toes at me, "shoes aren't allowed inside anymore."

"You woke me up to rag about my mom's being a clean-freak?" I asked, turning back on my side.

"No. I woke you so I wouldn't have to help your mom scrub the friggin' walls! And so *this time* I won't have changed my clothes and come all the way here and scrubbed the skin off my hands for *nothing*! And I woke you because I spent hours begging my dad to let me come, trying to convince him that I can handle it, and that I'm totally sane, and your cancer isn't flipping me out in the least. And I woke you to tell you about Amanda."

"Who?"

"That girl. The one I was telling you about, who's totally and completely torn up about you being sick, as long as people are watching. And if the people watching happen to be *boys*, then poor Amanda is the ultimate walking tragedy of suffering heartbreak."

"Amanda? Do I know an Amanda?" I asked, wondering for a second if the chemo had screwed up my brain.

"No, but what's that got to do with it?" Kay laughed.

"Huh?"

"Yep. She cries in the hall between classes, and constantly has to be comforted. Your cancer's probably the best thing that ever happened to her."

"Well, I'm glad someone's enjoying it," I said. "Maybe I can charge her a few bucks."

"Friday, I saw her in the lunch line," Kay said, jumping out of bed. She pretended she was Amanda, pushing her lunch tray down the cafeteria line, whistling.

"Then suddenly!" Kay said, clutching her chest, "Amanda just crumbles."

Kay made her legs go wiggly. "And the next thing you know, Amanda's in tears and is too, too stricken with sorrow to put her taco on her tray." Kay fluttered the back of her hand up to her forehead in a woe-is-me pose. "She was *that* worried about you."

"How do you know it was about *me*?" I asked.

"Oh, everyone knows," Kay said, settling back down on my bed.

"Wow," I said.

Kay nodded. "It's totally gross."

The sound of the vacuum cleaner got louder. Mom was right outside my door. Kay had to yell, "When are you coming back to school?"

"What day is it today?"

Kay rolled her eyes and said, "Sunday."

I was surprised. "Really?" I asked. "Then maybe tomorrow?"

"Good!" Kay said. "It's been horrible. Everyone constantly asks me about you and even the teachers are treating me weird. Mr. Hunter let me skip the quiz Friday."

"Why?"

"Because he knows we're best friends."

"So?"

Kay shrugged.

Then I got it. "Oh! Because he thinks I'm dying, right?"

Kay shrugged again.

"Does everyone think so?"

"Pretty much everyone." She nodded.

"Did you explain that I'm *not*?"

"Yeah, but you can tell they think I'm just being brave or stupid or in denial. They treat me like I'm mentally ill and made of glass."

"I'm sorry about that," I said.

Kay nodded again. "It's okay."

We listened to the vacuum for a while. And the more I thought about it, the creepier the idea of going back to school seemed.

"I thought I'd just, you know, *go back*," I said. "Like you'd go back after being out with the flu."

"Ha!" Kay spat. "They'll probably bring out a marching band and cheerleaders."

"As if I haven't vomited enough," I said.

We thought in silence again.

Then I said, "Yuck. I'm going to be the *cancer kid.*"

Kay frowned in agreement.

"Forget it, I'm not going."

"You've got to!" Kay whined. "Amanda *needs* you! Poor girl's a wreck!"

later, I joined my family at the dinner table for the first time in what felt like months.

"I'm so glad you're feeling better!" Mom said.

"What's that ugly stuff on your face?" my brother asked.

"Max!" Mom barked.

"What?" he yelled, throwing his fork onto his plate with a clatter. "It's not *my* fault Lizard's face is all messed up!"

"Bite me," I said. But I'd seen the marks too. Reddish lines and squiggles all over me; my legs, arms. But if Max wasn't allowed to mention them, they must *really* look bad.

"What do you think they are?" I asked my parents.

"I'll call and ask Heather tomorrow," Mom said.

"Who?"

"Heather," Mom said. "You remember her. That nice caseworker whose daughter plays soccer?"

"Soccer?"

"Izzy, you were sitting right there," Mom said.

"Whatever. I just want to know what these marks are all over me."

"They aren't so bad," my mom said. "Max was just being—"

"Honest," I said, ending her sentence.

Mom sighed. Then she changed the subject and asked if I thought I was ready to go back to school.

"How about homeschooling?" I asked.

Mom laughed. "What do *we* know about doing something like that?" she asked. "And anyway, it's not like I can quit my job."

"But I've got to get chemo again," I said with a shudder. "And I'll get even further behind, missing even *more* school to puke my guts out."

"Maybe not," Dad broke in. "Dr. Seacole said a significant number of cases get acclimated to the chemo and don't get as sick from subsequent treatments."

"Good, but still," I said. "At school I'd be the *cancer kid.*"

"I'm sure everyone will be nice," Mom said. "No one would pick on you for a thing like that."

I tried to explain. "I know they won't *pick* on me, but *nice* is bad enough. *Nice* makes my skin crawl."

She gave me her I-don't-know-what-you're-talking-about face.

"Like those letters from school," I tried to explain. "Most of them were from total strangers! They weren't writing to *me*, they were writing to the cancer."

"*Lymphoma*," Mom corrected.

"Kay says this one girl, Amanda, who I don't even know, is practically sobbing in the halls."

"I think that's sort of sweet," Mom said.

"Screw *sweet*," I said.

"*Izzy!*"

"Ask whatshername, the caseworker, about the marks on me and ask her about homeschool," I insisted, and left.

"Her name's Heather!" Mom called after me.

but there was no time for school, anyway. I had to go have scans for a "baseline." Heather told my mom, and my mom told me, that they'd repeat the same scans at the end of my treatment and compare them to see if the chemo worked.

"But I *had* a scan!" I said. "Remember that circle tube thing? Why don't they just use *that* as their baseline?"

"This must be different," Mom said with a shrug.

"One of the scans measures the sugars in your body and the other measures minerals," Dad said. "So they give two different views of the tumors."

"No way!" Max said. "Sugar and minerals? You told me her tumors were made of *cancer*."

Mom told Max to hush.

"Dr. Seacole explained it all to you, Izzy-pie," Dad said. "She even drew you pictures, remember?"

No one seemed to get it that I'd been a little distracted by agony and projectile vomiting back then.

In any case, I had to have an empty gut for the first scan, and that meant that I couldn't eat anything. And I had to drink this horrible laxative stuff.

"We'll go to any restaurant you want after the scan," Dad bribed.

I sniffed the bottle of laxative, and shook my head.

"Okay, two," he said. "You can choose where we have the next *two* dinners."

I held the bottle out for him to smell.

"You're a tough negotiator," he said. "My final offer is three."

"Make it four and we've got a deal," I said.

"No fair!" Max yelled. "*Lizard* picks the next *four* restaurants and *I* only got to pick *one* when I won the whole spelling bee?"

I gagged the swill down, took a dump, and considered myself done. I had no breakfast the next day, and spent the morning drawing food—pies mostly, but ice cream cones and cupcakes, too.

Mom had been crying less lately, but it turned out she'd just been refilling her tanks in preparation for our return trip to Children's. She began the second we backed down the driveway. Luckily, Dad drove this time.

We parked on the roof. The parking-lot staircase smelled like grape Benadryl, even through my sweaty paper mask. There was a mural painted in the stairwell of rabbits and flowers, and I touched the big red ladybug on a leaf for good luck.

The man at the front desk gave us orange stickers to wear and sent us to the Out Patient Tower, fifth floor, Oncology, Hematology.

Instead of turning right to go to the giraffe elevators, this time we turned left. All the smells were suddenly horribly familiar, although I have no idea what they were. Kids were everywhere, in various stages of messed-upness. Lots of bald and balding heads, green-and-white paper masks, scars and tubes and oxygen masks and wheelchairs or wheel-beds and IVs.

"Welcome to the house of horrors!" I said, but my parents were too rigid by then to react to anything I said.

After an obscenely long wait, a nurse called my name and led us into a dimly lit room full of beds and machines. She gave me a glass of poison Kool-Aid to drink. It was nasty, overly sweet stuff that gave my mouth the creeps.

A few years later, a young, kind of cute Latino guy had me lie down on the metal plank part of a hideous machine. He then tied me down with wide Velcro straps.

"Is this one of those magic tricks where you cut the girl in half?" I asked.

"That trick is nothing compared to this!" he said. "This one is truly hair-raising! But look! Nothing up my sleeves!" He pushed up his lab coat, flashing buff forearms.

"You must keep perfectly still," he said, making his voice go all showbiz, "while we scan every inch of your being, very, very slowly. We shall take pictures of your secret insides, from every angle, beginning at your feet and spiraling s-l-o-w-l-y up your body."

He pointed to a computer monitor that I could just see out of the corner of my eye. "Watch closely!" he said. "The image will be created before your very eyes! If that's not magic, I don't know what is."

He touched my head and said, "If you know how to meditate, this would be an excellent time to do so."

Then he was gone.

"Maybe he moonlights at the Hollywood Magic Castle between shifts," Dad said, which was the closest he'd come to cracking an actual joke at the hospital. Mom was too busy peering at the computer screen to react.

I, too, watched the image of my ankles, then leg bones gradually appearing on the monitor. It was drawn in millions of tiny dots: dense dots for bones, fewer dots for my flesh. Until then, I'd taken it on faith that my skeleton looked like the skeletons in science books—now I had proof.

There's something fascinating, in a creepy way, about seeing your own insides, but not for long. After a few minutes, it was just boring and uncomfortable. I had to ask Mom to scratch my nose and, of course, she only made it worse.

If anyone ever asked me to state one true thing, I'd say this: A person must scratch his or her own nose, if they want it scratched right.

To pass the time, I thought about where I'd make my parents take me to eat afterward. Maybe Tep Thai for chicken curry. Or how about Billy's Deli for cheese blintzes, or Buko for California rolls and tempura? No, we'd go straight to Frankie's for a veggie burger and a banana-raspberry smoothie.

But halfway through the scan, the magician tech switched off the machine, sat me up, and told me to go home and *really* empty out my system.

"There's too much bowel activity," he said.

"Huh?"

"Try drinking Fleet," he said.

"I did."

"Well, then try Ex-Lax and prune juice," he suggested. "And drink a lot of water. And don't eat anything but maybe clear soup."

How special that he and I are having this conversation, I thought.

"so, in other words, you're full of crap!" Kay hooted when I called her. "I could've told them that!"

"You're hilarious," I said. "So now I'm starving to death, and I can't eat because I have to go through the whole stupid thing again tomorrow!"

"Hey," Kay said, "my dad's out of town! Let me see if Mom'll let me go with you. You say the scan guy was hot?"

The phone clunked down. I heard Kay yelling for her mom in the background. Their house is huge. Eventually she clattered back onto the phone and, half out of breath, said, "Yes! I'm coming!"

By the next morning, I was so hungry I couldn't think of anything but food. I went through the same everything: drive, wait around with my fellow chemo-sapiens, lie down, get strapped in, be zapped—but this time, Kay was there and the technician guy was satisfied with the emptiness of my bowels. I was so proud.

Afterward, we went to Eatz Diner because it was close to the hospital, and I was way too hungry to drive any farther. I chowed down on a tuna-Swiss club on toasted sourdough, with nachos, a chocolate shake, and mixed-berry pie a la mode.

Then we took off for the beach. Well, first Kay and I begged and pleaded. I acted pitifully cancer-ridden, and Kay made her sad-eyed-puppy face.

"We don't have towels or suits or a blanket or anything," Mom said. "We don't even have sunblock."

"Afraid I'll get skin cancer?" I teased.

"And I have to be back to pick up your brother at three," Mom added.

"No problem!" I assured her. "We'll just have a quick peek, maybe stick our toes in the water for a second, and zoom home."

Mom finally agreed, with a sigh.

It was a long, stinky freeway ride to Santa Monica, with traffic slowing to a sweaty crawl through downtown. But eventually, the temperature cooled and the beautiful fishy smell of the sea knocked the last puffs of stale hospital air out of us.

Because it was a school day for the rest of the world, the parking lots were empty. I'd never seen that before.

Kay and I charged across the hot sand and shrieked into the freezing surf with all our clothes on. We dove and bobbed in and out of the waves, tumbling every which way with the salty tide. The only sounds were the crashing waves, the screaming gulls, and us.

Eventually, I noticed Mom sitting in the sand. *Oops.*

But when we hauled ourselves out of the water, blue-lipped and breathless, and plopped down next to her, Mom didn't lecture us or rag about our broken promise. She had her face tipped up to the sun and she was smiling. She told us she'd called Riley's mom to pick up Max after school, so we could take our time.

When we were dry, we climbed up to the pier. There were no lines at any of the rides, so the three of us rode the Ferris wheel again and again. The old guy running it gave us a free, extra-long ride the last time.

We searched the horizon for whales from up there, squinting into the setting sun, half blinded by the twinkling waves. Kay swore she saw a whole herd of dolphins.

"We should skip school more often," she said, back in the car. Then she fell asleep instantly. Mom and I talked quietly so we wouldn't wake her. We talked about someday renting a beach house on one of the walking streets so we could stick our feet in the sand day or night without having to get in a car.

"I'd get up at dawn," I told her, "to scout for shells and driftwood and stuff that the tide spits out."

"Ha!" Mom laughed. "You at dawn." She leaned over and gave my leg a little poke. "That would be something to see."

kay considered herself my good-luck charm. But her dad was on his way home, so she couldn't come to watch them inject radioactive dye into me for the next day's scan. This time, I remembered to bring my notebook and pen, to kill the time spent waiting.

Beside the random wheelchairs and rolling beds of seriously gorked patients, the radiology waiting room always had two boys at the video-game controls, fighting to the death onscreen without saying a word to each other in real life. They were never the same two boys, but they were always boys.

The stacks of coloring-book pages of Disney princesses were for the ungorked girls. They sat at low round tables, shyly sharing crayons. I was tempted to join them and color a bright yellow dress on Belle, but I was too big for the chairs. I had to sit along the wall, like a mom.

I didn't feel like wondering how sick any of those kids were. I didn't want to smile at the little girls in party dresses and pretend there was nothing bad going on. I didn't want to wonder, even for a second, which one, or ones, of them—of us—weren't going to make it. So I doodled.

I drew the clock, the chair (until someone sat in it). I copied the Spanish sign on the wall that showed a baby wearing the ever-popular green-and-white paper mask. But that was about it. There just weren't many things to draw that weren't awful.

I tried to get my mom to play Twenty Questions, but she couldn't concentrate. Every time a name was called, she'd jump and lose count. Hard to believe she was the same mom who'd been so relaxed and normal at the beach just yesterday. It was as if it had never happened, or happened so long ago and far away that time had twisted it out of shape.

Mom apologized for being bad company, but I said, "Next time I need a scan, I'm going to make Aunt Lucy bring me."

Burn.

finally, it was my turn, but the guy who prepped me for the scan was a total dork-wad.

"Do you have a PICC line?" he asked me.

I was so sick of that question. I wanted to wear a sign that said *NO PICC LINE and NOT sorry!* But I just said no.

"It would make things so much easier for both of us," he said.

Bite me, I did not say.

It took *five* excruciating stabs before this dipshit found my vein. And he spent the whole time muttering about the damn PICC line. My mom's hand on my shoulder was more to keep me from decking the jerk than to comfort me from the pain he was causing.

Then he put Valium in my IV and it chilled me right out. That wasn't why he gave it to me, though. It was something about Valium's helping the body absorb the dye.

I felt loopy and belted out Disney songs until the woman monitoring the scan told me that if I moved too much, we'd have to start all over.

Mom, of course, tried to make conversation with her, and learned that the woman was still in training. She complained about how hard it was to work these hours with two little kids at home.

Mom asked how old her children were.

"Ten and twelve," she said. "Both girls."

Mom asked if she ever brought her daughters to work.

The woman wrinkled her nose and, sweeping her hand in a gesture that included the computers, the machine, and, of course, *me*, said, "Nooo, I wouldn't want them to see *this*. It would frighten them." And she gave a little shudder at the idea of her children being exposed to such a sight.

Mom looked like she'd been slapped, but she didn't tell the woman off. And I didn't, either, much as I would've liked to. It wasn't worth moving and having to repeat the entire scan. And by the time we were done, I just wanted to get the hell out of there.

As we were leaving, the first dork told me not to be around pregnant women if I could help it, because I was now radioactive. He also told me to flush twice after I used the toilet so I wouldn't radiate whoever went after me. I would have thought he was joking except that he wasn't a jokey kind of guy.

After the scan, Mom suggested dropping me off at school for the rest of the day. But I said that would be socially irresponsible. "What if I accidentally dribble toxic pee on one of my pregnant classmates, Mom? Wouldn't you feel awful?"

She sighed, and turned the car toward Griffith Park.

We hadn't been there in ages, although when Max was little, we constantly went there for the pony rides. This was different. The parking lot was deserted. The ponies weren't out; the merry-go-round was locked up. There was no drum circle, no dueling boom boxes, no picnic litter overflowing the trash cans. The only sound was birds.

Mom and I drifted around as if we were the last people on Earth, until we practically tripped over a homeless guy asleep in the shade of a massive oak. Two white butterflies fluttered around him.

back home, everyone who called made basically the same joke about my glowing in the dark. I slept the rest of the day, thanks to the Valium, I guess.

The next morning, Mom didn't try to wake me in her old way; she did it gently, to *ask* if I was going to school. I said no. And she tiptoed out of my room, closing the door softly behind her. *Ahhh! The silver lining.*

when I woke up, there were voices in the living room. I staggered out and found Mom surrounded by towering stacks of books. She was scrubbing the empty bookcases. Aunt Lucy was there, eating pita sandwiches off a tray. She had Pupkin's undivided attention.

My aunt patted the couch next to her. "Just in time for a late lunch, sleepyhead," she said.

"That's the one good thing about cancer," I replied.

"*Lymphoma*," Mom corrected.

Aunt Lucy looked from me to Mom and said, "Know what that reminds me of?"

Mom and I shook our heads.

My aunt handed me a sandwich and poured me some lemonade, saying, "Remember back in the eighties, or I don't know, nineties, maybe? Some folks with nothing better to do decided that calling the astrological sign *Cancer* was too harsh and negative. Remember that, Helen?"

Mom said no.

"Of course you do!" Aunt Lucy said, exasperated by my mom's memory. "It was sort of Politically Correct meets hippie New Age?"

Mom was wiping down each book and replacing it on the freshly washed shelf. "Doesn't ring a bell," she said with a shrug.

"Well," my aunt went on, "they tried to change the word *Cancer* in the horoscopes to *Moon Child*. Like, Gemini, Aquarius, *Moon Child* . . ."

I laughed, planning to draw sixties paisley, psyche-delic peace-sign doodles as soon as I finished eating.

"Seriously," Aunt Lucy insisted, "you two could compromise and call it Moon Child disease. How's that?"

Mom flicked the dust cloth at her sister.

Aunt Lucy ducked, then turned to me and said, "It's so you, Izzy! Tying daisy chains and frolicking in a field of wildflowers, wearing a poufy dress." She leaned over and touched the tip of my nose. "Our Izzy Moon Child."

I snapped at her finger.

the next time I saw Kay, she seemed more obsessed with hating Amanda than ever. She was prac-tically seething when she said, "Amanda says she's making a *funny* get-well video for you, because she believes in laugh therapy."

"Funny's good," I said.

Kay growled at me. "Funny? Funny is stupid!" she said. "Funny's beyond stupid."

"You're funny," I said.

Kay leaned over and gave me a shove. "Amanda is a dufus. She wouldn't know funny if it punched her in the face."

I squinted at Kay, trying to see why she hated Amanda so much. "Amanda didn't give me cancer, you know," I tried.

"Yes, she did!" Kay shot back. "She totally did!"

"No, I'm pretty sure it was that baby-talking social worker in the hospital. And Ms. Lyons, the PE demon," I said. "For sure she gave it to me. And how about that saleslady who accused me of stealing that stupid ring?"

Kay nodded. "But mostly Amanda."

"And homework and pop quizzes," I said. "I bet they're carcinogenic."

"Actually, you know what totally, totally causes all kinds of diseases?" Kay asked. "I mean *besides* Amanda?"

I said, "What?"

"Alarm clocks! Getting up *alarmed* every school day. I'm positive that if we woke when we were ready, and school started at a reasonable time—say, noon—we'd all be as healthy and happy as Pupkin."

Pupkin thumped his tail on the floor at the mention of his name.

"But that's in addition to Amanda," Kay added.

I said, "Right." But I was thinking that Amanda may be a drama queen, but some kids I thought of as my *friends* hadn't called or come over, or made any videos. That sucked worse than the thought of some loser running around trying to get attention off my bad luck.

"I haven't heard a peep from Penelope," I said. "What's up with that?"

Kay looked at her cuticles. "Pen's all screwed up over this," she said. "She says she doesn't know what to say to you."

"And Mica?" I asked. "Hard to imagine Mica tongue-tied."

"He and Becca came to the hospital, remember?" Kay asked. "You puked for them. Several times, in fact."

"So they're going to hold a grudge over a little thing like that?" I asked. "God, if I stopped calling or visiting everyone who ever threw up on me—"

Kay laughed. "People are such turds," she said. "But now I've got to go because it's a school night and my mom'll go nuts. See? It's that early-to-bed, early-to-rise crap again!"

kay came over after school the next day. "My dad thinks I'm at the library," she said.

"Why does he hate me so much?" I asked.

"He doesn't!" Kay said, turning red. "It's not like that." Then she got busy greeting Pupkin and letting him lick her face. "So," Kay said, changing the subject, "guess what good old Amanda did today."

"I give up."

"She brought a camera to school to film her quote, unquote *funny* video. She didn't ask *me*, or *Penelope* or any of your actual *friends* to be in it, though," Kay said. "She just shot the people she most wanted to impress with how *sensitive* she is. It totally bugged the crap out of me."

I didn't know why this Amanda was getting off on my cancer like that, but it didn't bother me like it did Kay. What was bothering me at the moment was the amount of hair that had fallen out in the shower.

I ran my fingers through my hair to see what would happen and felt a jolt of white panic. I placed a handful of brown strands on the table in front of Kay.

"Oh, no!" she said. "Already?"

I combed my fingers through again and added another fistful of hair to the first.

"Stop it!" Kay said. "Maybe if you don't *pull* it like that. Anyone can rip . . ."

Among the gifts that had been piling up was a bunch of hats and bandannas. I guess everyone knew this was coming. I dropped a third handful.

"Okay, okay, I get it," Kay said, and we both stared at the clump of hair on the table.

"You know," she said, "I heard about this one kid who lost her hair, and all her friends and relatives and stuff shaved their heads so she wouldn't feel alone. I'd totally do that if you want."

I added a fourth handful. I just couldn't stop.

"Also," Kay said, "there's this place my mom told me about, where people donate their hair to make into wigs for cancer patients. You could get a cute one. Curls. Whatever."

No matter how many times I dragged my fingers through, more hair came away easily. I wondered how soon I'd have actual bald spots, if I didn't already. And how soon it would be completely gone.

Kay reached out and touched my hair. She added some to the pile.

"I've seen kids at the hospital with thin, wispy old-man hair," I told Kay. "It looks gross. I'd rather have none at all. Then I'd wear big dangling earrings and lots of eye makeup, and look dramatic and artistic."

"Super-dark sunglasses and trailing silk scarves," Kay added. "Very cool. A lot of models wear shaved heads."

Suddenly, Kay jumped up and shrieked. "I've got it! It's perfect! We *tell* Amanda that we're doing the group head-shave thing. Tell her we're *all* going to shave our heads to support you—me, Becca, Mica, Penelope, and everyone—and then we *don't!* Get it? We just don't! And she'll show up at school the next day, the *only* one with a shaved head! Do you love it?"

We laughed together for a while, but then I had to add, "Well, besides *me*," I reminded her. "I'll be bald, too. I don't think I'm going to have a lot of choice on this one."

Kay sat back down. "Poop," she said. "That totally ruins it."

I said, "Sorry."

Then I asked the question that was on my mind. "If everyone knows about my cancer thing, that means Jared knows, too, right?"

Kay said, "I suppose."

"He could have called or something," I said. "It wouldn't have killed him."

"He's a turd ball. I don't know what you see in him, I swear," Kay mumbled.

"Has he said *anything* to you about me?" I asked.

"Izz, he's a total jerk," Kay said, without looking me in the eye.

"Okay," I demanded. "What aren't you telling me?"

"Nothing."

I gave her a look.

Kay ducked under the table to hide.

"Fess up," I said. "You'll feel better."

"It's too stupid for words," Kay said from the floor. "Way too stupid."

I waited, playing with the wad of hair.

Finally, Kay's voice came up through the table. "Jared and Amanda are going out," she said. "There, now you know."

I let that sink in. Then, "Jeez." No wonder Kay hated Amanda so much.

Kay crawled back onto her chair. "Those two turds deserve each other," she said. "Let them rot."

But all I could think was, *jeez*. That so totally sucks it isn't even funny.

{ SEVEN }

no one in my pictures had hair anymore. Hair, I decided, was unnecessary. I found myself drawing long rows of dancing bald people, trailing transfusion and IV tubes like umbilical cords. And bald-headed balloon people, held by IV kite string.

Cheery art!

Kay said I should have an art show at school. Dad thought my drawings could be auctioned off to rich people to raise money for cancer research. Aunt Lucy said that if they were analyzed by a shrink, I'd probably be locked away forever in a rubber room.

Except for the picture I'd given to my hospital roommate, Carrie, nothing left my notebook. I wouldn't even let myself tear out the ones that really stunk. I could scribble them out, if I had to, but they couldn't leave.

heather told Mom that the red marks all over me were from one of the antinausea meds I'd been given in the hospital. One of the drugs that *hadn't* worked. She said it makes your skin so delicate that it rips under the surface. That didn't explain the scratches all over my face or the hieroglyphics on my arms and legs, until I remembered that during my chemo-puking-fest, I'd scratched like mad. The marks must've been from my own fingernails.

Mom asked Heather how long they'd last, and she said, "Some of them might fade in time," which meant: the rest *wouldn't*.

And, as if that weren't depressing enough, Heather made an appointment for my next chemotherapy. This one would be outpatient, meaning I wouldn't stay overnight.

I had to have blood tests first, to make sure I had enough white blood cells.

"And if I don't have enough?" I asked.

"I guess we go home and try when you're stronger," Mom said.

"And I get stabbed both times?"

Mom winced. "Maybe we should've let them put in that PICC line. They said it would spare you a lot of pokes."

"I told them not to," I said.

"So did we," Dad said. "You seemed so set against it."

Well, that explained why I woke with no PICC. It was probably my parents, not me, the hospital staff had listened to. At least my parents had stood up for me.

I thanked them.

"Don't be silly," Dad said.

"If I could take the disease into my body instead, I would," Mom said. "And if I could . . ." But she ended her sentence with a sigh.

The other thing caseworker Heather told my mom was that it would be best for me to get back to normal life, meaning *school*, as soon as possible. Kay was thrilled. I was not.

"I think it'd be better to come back while you've still got some hair," Kay said over the phone.

"Then I better hurry," I said, plucking stray strands off my shirt.

Mom and Kay wanted me to go Wednesday. I wanted me to go never. We compromised on Friday. That way, I'd have a weekend to freak out if I had to, before having to face it again Monday.

friday came in a blink. Mom woke me, then woke me again, and again. It wasn't as violent as in the old days, but I could tell she meant business.

I stood a long time in the shower, trying to remember how I used to feel before school. All I knew for sure was that this was different.

Mom caught me peering in the mirror at the streaks on my face. "You only see them because you're looking for them," she said. "They're hardly noticeable. Just put on a little concealer."

I pulled my hair back in a ponytail—a thin ponytail—and checked to see how much scalp showed. Red marks and bald spots were definitely *not* my usual morning concerns.

Kay had convinced her mom to drop her at my house in the morning so we could ride the same bus in. It began the second we got to the bus stop. Hyper-gonzo ADHD Trevor Nelson stared meekly at his shoes and toed a pebble in the dirt, quiet as a bug. Next, Melinda Whatshername ran up and gave me a hug, then apologized for hugging me so hard. Even the bus driver knew. I could tell by the way she said, "Good morning."

I sat next to Kay and tried to crack a joke about it, but she looked ready to explode. I nudged her with my elbow. "Hey," I said. "You okay?" And she just growled, "Grrr!"

Had my backpack always been this heavy, and the halls so noisy? I took out a notebook to doodle in, and saw the drawing of emo-Nina overdoing her sonnet in drama. I studied it, wondering if I was still the same girl who'd drawn it.

Everyone in all my classes and in the hall was as nice as humanly possible, which was eerie. Like being back at school—but not quite the *same* school. Not that anyone used to be mean, but this was different, all this smiling and nodding and helloing. There was something spooky and science-fictiony about it.

Plus, every single one of my teachers told me that I didn't have to do any work unless I felt like it. I decided to take them at their word.

Maybe some Moon Children feel differently, but here's what I figured: Having cancer and getting chemo was bad enough without homework and exams on top of it.

And if, out of pity or sympathy or superstition or kindness or guilt or *whatever*, my teachers were offering me passing grades to sit home eating M&M's and watching Comedy Central, I was accepting. And I was ready to start accepting *immediately*.

Too bad the same offer wasn't made to the cancer kid's best friend, though, because when I saw Kay in the hall between classes, she looked so crazed, I practically expected her to snap in half. No wonder her father was worried.

Maybe I was just paranoid, but it seemed to me that my friends acted even stranger than the strangers did. Penelope tried to act like nothing was weird at first, and *that* was weird. Becca, who was quiet to start with, was freakishly silent. Mica tried way too hard to rhyme *nympho*maniac with *lympho*maniac in joke after joke. And Kay—forget Kay, she was a total mess.

At lunch, we sat at our usual table, but it all seemed like a bad play where no one knew their lines or cues. At one point, Penelope said, "What do they think caused it? I mean, it's not like you're a *smoker* or anything."

And Kay barked, "Not all cancers are from smoking."

When we were in the hospital, Mom had asked Dr. Seacole the same thing. "We live fairly close to the power lines," Mom said. "Or could it have been the brush fires? They swept so close to our house that our sky stayed gray and snowed ash for days."

Dr. Seacole had raised her hand, making her bangles jangle. "This line of thinking can only make you crazy," she said. "We do not know what is the cause of this. One day, yes, we will have an explanation, but now, no. I only can encourage you to spare yourself this questioning."

If I'd had my hospital notebook with me, I would've shown Penelope a drawing I'd done a few nights ago. It was a swirling composite of all the things I could remember ever being told cause cancer. The nitrates in hot dogs; other fast-food preservatives; spray paint; hair spray; bug spray; burnt meat; first- and secondhand cigarette, pipe, and cigar smoke; cleaning stuff; paint thinner; insecticide; car, bus, and airplane exhaust; forest fires; industrial pollution; nail polish; glue; and I can't remember what else, all in a big, pretty tumor.

"Hey, Kay," I said, "remember when we were, like, nine, and we wanted to be the tattooed ladies in our imaginary circus?"

Kay nodded down at her stuffed potato boat, the only halfway decent thing in the cafeteria.

I told the others, "We got a bunch of Kay's mom's permanent markers and drew all over ourselves. Actually, Kay gave up way before I did. She said it was because she was a lousy artist. But probably she was just a wuss even back then, and afraid of getting in trouble."

I gave Kay a little shove, but she just quarter-smiled at her untouched potato.

"I went wild, though. Forehead-to-toenails with a long purple swirl curling around my belly button, and down both legs like a vine. Flowers up my arms and fingers. I even decorated my ears. Remember?"

Kay nodded a tiny bit.

"I thought it was *beautiful*," I continued, "but our moms didn't. We were grounded for as long as it took to wear off, which was a long, l-o-n-g time."

Kay finally cracked a half-assed smile.

"I bet those markers were toxic," I said, making her swallow her smile in one gulp.

Mica shoved the last wad of his sandwich into his mouth and said, "The fact is, Izz, you must've done something really bad in a former life."

The rest of us watched him chew awhile, until he added, "That's how it works, you know. You're being punished for your evil past."

I laughed, sort of.

"Get serious," Penelope said.

"I am!" Mica answered.

Becca didn't say a word.

Leaving the cafeteria afterward, I whispered, "Boy, *that* was fun." But Kay was done smiling.

in fifth hour, a boy named Andy Siegel, who sat in front of me and was an all-A student, turned around and said, "Want some of my notes or something, on the stuff you missed?"

I shrugged. "Nah," I said. "I think I'm just going to dare them to flunk me."

He laughed and gave me a thumbs-up. Then later, he turned around and laughed again. I don't know what he was laughing about, exactly, but it made me laugh a little, too. And that was my singular, only, isolated laugh of the entire day.

i stopped in the restroom before History, to make sure there was no food in my teeth or boogers hanging out of my nose or whatever. Then I got to class and there was *Jared*, as adorable and blue-eyed as ever. He bobbed his head at me and said, "Hey," and I melted.

But before I said anything back, he'd turned and loped away.

Then, after class, I saw him with his arm around someone short. I looked closer. Oh, *that* Amanda! I cracked up that *she* was the one who'd missed me so badly and was making the movie and all. I knew her— she was a total brain-free ditzoid!

Kay didn't see what was so funny about that, or anything else. Her annoying new stiffness was getting on my nerves. Was it my job to help *Kay* through *my* cancer?

Forget it. The easiest thing would be just to hibernate. Hide. Lie low till the storm passed. Everything was just a little too weird, or a *lot* too weird. I wanted to go home and stay there forever, or at least until I was old enough to move to some gorgeous tropical island where I could lie in a hammock all day, being served fancy drinks by half-naked boys with gorgeous bodies and great tans. Was that too much to ask?

then came the sores in my mouth. At first I thought I'd bitten my cheek, or somehow got a paper cut, but then I remembered the Smurf telling me about mouth sores.

Was it necessary that I have *every* possible side effect from chemotherapy? Couldn't I just skip a few?

No. And the sores soon got so nasty that I could eat only the wimpiest nonfoods imaginable without pain. Worse, I was now forced to gargle a pink glop twice a day that was so foul that not even Pupkin would touch it. I know that for a *fact.*

mom asked Heather about the rash I got on my hands. It turned out to be a creeping fungus. *Nice.* She asked Heather about the ringing in my ears and my blurry vision and the shooting pains I still had in my arms. Heather said it was all normal. My collection of pills, swills, and goos grew to cover the entire bathroom counter.

Mom asked Heather if I should be taking megavitamins since I was so weak and sleepy. But Heather said that anything that made me stronger made the cancer stronger, too. "We want Isabelle's body to be a hostile environment," she said.

My body, the *hostile environment.* She got that right.

mom quoted Heather the way born-agains quote the Bible, and she called her constantly for advice. Unfortunately, Heather thought I should stay in school.

"What about all the germs?" I asked Mom. "No one's bleaching anything there."

"Heather told me to tell you that if anyone is coughing or sneezing near you in class, you should ask the teacher to move you," Mom said.

"But I heard colds are most contagious before you have any symptoms," I said, hearing myself whine. "So I could be sitting next to a total germ-bomb and not know it."

"Well," Mom said, "Heather thinks the psychological benefits of having a normal life are worth the risk. And you can always wear your mask, just in case."

"Sure. That'll feel normal."

i went into the kitchen in search of baby mush— rice pudding or yogurt. My brother looked up and said, "Do you mind? I'm *eating*."

I said, "So?"

"So, your hair is grossing me out," he explained. "Can't you wear a hat or something?"

My mom wasn't in the room to scold him.

I said, "Know what? You're the only honest one left."

Max looked suspicious. When I reached over to nab a spoon out of the dish drainer, he ducked, thinking I was going to slug him.

"For real," I said.

so Kay sneaked over after school and cut what was left of my hair really short, and that helped. It was thin, but it still looked like hair. I got a lot of compliments on it the next day at school, but that didn't mean much.

That guy in my fifth hour, Andy Siegel, turned around in his seat and told me that when his sister's hair got thin, she shaved it off and started wearing tiaras and crowns.

"Your sister lost her hair?" I asked, shocked.

He nodded.

"How old is she?" I asked.

"Well, now she's twenty-two," he said. "She's a junior at UCLA. But she lost her hair back when she still lived at home. She was, I don't know, seventeen?"

Wow!

I spent the rest of the class period drawing Andy's bald sister in her crown, with all her long-haired subjects bowing at her royal feet. I looked up from my drawing to study the back of Andy's head from time to time.

All the bald kids I knew of were at Children's, as if that were the only place they existed. But Andy was someone from the outside world—from *my* outside world. I loved his sister, whoever she was. And I could not believe how little I'd noticed Andy before.

in my former life, Mom said I could dye my hair any color I wanted, as soon as I brought home a perfect report card. That was the same as saying I'd never be allowed to dye my hair . . . ever.

But now, the rules were more fluid. "I'll go to school if I can dye my hair peacock blue," I told her.

Mom sighed.

"It'll all be gone soon, anyway," I said.

Mom sighed again and said she'd ask Heather.

The good news was that Heather said it was okay as long as I used temporary dye. The bad news was that they were out of peacock blue.

I looked at the bright pink and the orange but decided they were too girlie. "I really had my heart set on blue," I said.

Kay showed me a dark blue.

"Bor-ring," I said.

"No! It's like Veronica's hair from the *Archie* comics," Kay said. "And Veronica always got Archie away from poor Betty, even though Betty was blond."

"Veronica was filthy rich," I said. "And Archie was a dweeb."

"Superman's hair is blue," Max said, trying to be part of things.

Kay put down the dark blue and rattled a box of green. "This'll be perfect for Saint Patty's day," she said.

"Lizards are supposed to be green," Max added. Then he asked my mom if he could dye his hair, too.

"Not until *you* get cancer," I told him, making his eyes go huge.

"Izzy!" Mom gasped. "What a thing to say!"

I asked the salesgirl when she thought they'd get more peacock blue, but I knew that at the rate my hair was going, whatever she said would be too late.

The girl cracked her gum and said, "Maybe three weeks?"

Kay shook the box of green again. It was a bright Kelly green.

I said, "Fine."

I could tell it pained my mom to pay for hair dye, but she did it with only a moderate amount of sighing, which was nice.

It turned out green was not my color, though. And the dye stained my scalp so it looked like I'd scribbled on my head with green marker. Not quite the look I'd had in mind.

{ EIGHT }

then it was time for the next chemo.

Max left for school in a snit. "Lizard, Lizard, Lizard, that's all anyone cares about!" he said. He was pissed because he'd have to go home with his friend Riley. But Riley had every kind of junk food imaginable, and normally Max *begged* to go there.

The drive to Children's was very familiar. Same freeways, overpasses, drunks, and strip clubs. Mom felt superstitiously drawn to the karma seller on Sunset but he wasn't there. The hospital parking lot was full. Big day for sick kids, I guess. Dad had to drop us.

Mom and I got our orange stickers and found the place in the day hospital where I had to register. They gave me a gray plastic card that looked like a credit card. Gee! My own chemo card!

We were sent to Triage, where we waited forever in the waiting room with many, many other families. Most of them spoke Spanish, thwarting Mom's impulse to talk to strangers.

We stared at the curling paper cutouts of Disney characters taped to the walls. They looked like they'd been colored with crayons long ago. Piglet was there, and Eeyore.

One young-looking mom had three little boys with her. It was easy to tell which one was the patient. He was the one who looked spaced-out, sitting still while his brothers bumped into everyone and fought with each other and whined about being hungry, thirsty, bored, tired, and having to make wee-wee.

A nurse finally called me in to take my *vitals*. Which is what those of us with chemo cards call our vital signs—weight, pulse, blood pressure, height.

Next I was sent downstairs for *labs*. That was another one of those cute medical nicknames for those of us on the inside.

"Hey! Maybe I can get language credit for speaking Hospital!" I said to my parents.

Neither of them even smiled.

"Pupkin's a lab," I tried next. "Wouldn't that rock? If they sent the Moon Children down to play with a bunch of Labrador puppies to chill them out before chemo?"

My dad gave me a half smile. Mom just blinked back tears.

I'd forgotten my notebook, but I could imagine the drawing perfectly; happy bald-headed babies on IV leashes. A big doctor holding all the dog leashes and kid leashes in his latex-gloved hand.

But there were no puppies in the blood lab. An Asian nurse with spiky blond hair took me into a room and asked me if I had a PICC line.

Hisss.

She looked at my veins. One arm after the other, then back to the first. My arms started to throb with pain, from fingertip to shoulder, before she'd even picked her target.

Ah! I thought, This must be the mental illness bonus for kids with chemo cards! Feeling the pain *before* the stab!

Mom was explaining how much trouble everyone had getting blood out of me as an inpatient.

The nurse nodded but didn't look impressed. She said the same needle-poke would be for the blood work first and the chemotherapy later. "But if your bloods are too low for you to get treatment today, we'll just take it out," she said.

Another nurse came in, pushing a wheelchair with a very thin, weak-looking girl in it, maybe my age, maybe a little younger. She had the same blank-eyed expression as the boy in the waiting room. I wondered if they were stoned on pain medication. Stoned on *pain?*

"Mind if we share the room?" her nurse asked. We didn't mind.

The nurse had the girl get up and lean over the examining table. She lifted the girl's shirt, showing her ribs and the pointy bumps of her spine. They were like the bones of some animal who'd starved to death in the desert. Her flesh, the dark sand blown in thin drifts over the bones. At least that was how I would've drawn it if I knew how to draw a whole lot better than I really did.

I watched the nurse squeeze a tube of something white on the girl's brown back. She put a pad over the goo, and taped it in place. Then she pulled the girl's shirt back down and helped her back into the wheelchair, and they left. The girl hadn't made a sound.

My nurse was now studying the veins in the back of my hand. I asked her what the gunk on the girl's back was for, and she said, "It's numbing gel. She's getting a spinal."

Mom gasped.

"What's that?" I asked.

"It's a diagnostic tap, where they extract some spinal fluid."

"With a needle?" I asked, instantly feeling an eerie tingle in my spine.

The nurse nodded. Then she thumped a vein and said, "I'm going to try this one. Do you want cold spray?"

I didn't know what cold spray was.

"It sort of freezes the area. Want to try it?"

She'd already tied the tourniquet around my arm and was having me make a fist. "Yes! Try it!" I said.

I gripped mom's fingers as hard as I could with my free hand, and buried my face in her side. I heard and felt the spray, and it *was* cold. A weird kind of cold that wasn't like ice.

Then the nurse said, "Keep really still now. One . . ." I took a deep breath. "Two. Three."

Cold or not—it hurt. Mom exhaled along with me in a *whoosh*. I figured that meant it had worked. "Don't look yet," Mom said.

The nurse kept doing stuff, taping one thing, bandaging another, I don't know, I didn't look. Then she said, "Next time, be sure to drink water before you come. It opens up your veins a little and makes it easier."

I told myself I'd drink a gallon. Two!

the nurse said we had an hour until they'd have the results of my blood test.

My parents and I were back out in the hall.

"Hungry?" Dad asked.

I remembered my old roommate, Carrie, saying there was a cafeteria in the basement. And there was a McDonald's off the lobby, which seemed weird for a hospital. I guess they figure, hell, what's a few more fries? The kids are already sick.

The third choice was to actually *leave* the hospital. Go out into the real world and eat real food. We were all wearing our orange o.p.t.5 (Out Patient Tower, fifth floor) stickers, and I had a needle in my vein that was attached to a tube taped to my bandaged arm. I couldn't quite imagine mixing the two worlds—outside and in. On the other hand, staying there for a whole hour when I didn't *have* to was insane.

If only I could go into suspended animation, I thought. Wake me when it's over—and not until.

But we rode down to the cafeteria. There was no way we could pretend to be anywhere else; practically everyone wore lab coats or scrubs or nursing uniforms, with stethoscopes or surgical masks around their necks. The few nonmedical-looking people seemed lost, like me and my parents—wandering from food station to food station, holding empty trays.

The only things for sale that wouldn't hurt my mouth were yogurt and soup, and I was sick to death of both. Plus, I was already losing weight—from my boobs mostly, which figures.

After we sat down, two people took the table next to us. The woman was crying. When people in Children's Hospital cry, it's probably not over a broken nail or boyfriend trouble. The lady's husband or brother, or whatever he was, had puffy red eyes, too, and a sniffly nose, although he wasn't crying at that exact second.

I could see Mom thinking, *Who does that woman think she is, trying to outcry me? Ha! You want tears? I'll show you tears! Watch and learn!* And the pro let rip with an awesome display. Dad patted her hand and stared into his coffee. It was way fun.

I suggested we go for a walk. Screw my earlier confusion about mixing the two worlds. *This* world sucked, and we needed to get the hell out while we could. Griffith Park was nearby. I remembered the homeless man, asleep peacefully under that big, old tree. All his earthly possessions in a tidy pile beside him. I wished I were him.

Mom looked at her watch. I knew she was afraid to leave the hospital, afraid we'd come back late and get in trouble. Maybe they'd say, *No chemo for you, young lady! Only good little girls who wait patiently in the waiting rooms deserve to be cured.*

But Mom finally agreed to go outside, as long as we just walked in tight circles around the hospital. It was hardly a nature break, but at least it smelled different outside.

"Maybe we should head back," Mom said almost instantly.

Dad told her we still had at least fifteen minutes, but Mom power-sighed until she won.

no one was ready for us yet, so I went to the pay phone in the hall and called Kay. "Is the chemo over?" she asked.

"It hasn't even started," I answered.

"So you could've come to school today, you faker!" Kay said. "You just didn't want anyone to see your green hair!"

"Yeah, right," I said. "Like this is *way* more fun than school. I've been sitting around here since dawn—getting stabbed."

"Ick," Kay sympathized. "Well, you didn't miss anything. It was a stupid day."

"Here, too," I said. "I'm waiting for the results of my blood test. If it comes back bad, I won't have to get chemo. Keep your fingers crossed."

"Okay," Kay said. "Call me when you get home, and maybe my mom'll bring me over."

eventually, we were put in a white examining room to wait and wait for my oncologist. The only paper any of us had for me to draw on was the tiny receipt from our basement lunch. The view out the window was of parking and trash bins. I went through the drawers to kill time, but there was nothing that interesting. Rubber gloves in three sizes, gauze, tape, disposable thermometers. Mom flew into a panic, afraid I'd get arrested for snooping, I guess.

When Dr. Seacole finally walked in, I thought, Oh yeah, I remember her. She was the one with all the necklaces and the Jamaican accent and the mini sidekick. Dr. Seacole felt my neck, looked in my nose and mouth, listened to me breathe, and told me my blood was fine.

Shit.

Back to the waiting room until a blond nurse named Cathy Dooley led us to a room with four beds, each facing a different direction. Three beds had kids in them. Every bed had a TV hanging over it, and all of them were on—including the one over the bed that was waiting for me. I looked up and saw the Teletubbies dancing around.

Cathy was arranging her tray and talking to my mom.

"Aren't you going to wear the Smurf outfit?" I asked her.

"Nah," she said. "I hate that thing." And she handed me sheets of paper about all my drugs. I'm not sure why. Maybe so I could sing along.

The first kind of chemo was the Vinblastine, which had among its list of possible side effects, *low blood counts, constipation, abdominal pain, nausea, vomiting, loss of appetite, irritation to the nerves causing tingling, numbness or muscle weakness of hands or feet, difficulty urinating, jaw pain, rash, skin sensitivity to sunlight, hair loss.*

Nice.

But at the time, the only shitty part was that my arm, where the needle was, felt like it had been slammed in a door. Luckily it was my left hand. I flipped over the sheet of paper describing my meds and drew on the back with the hospital crayons. They were crappy crayons but better than nothing.

After the Vinblastine came the red one, Adriamycin. I colored the back of the sheet that explained the possible side effects that came free with all of them: good old nausea, vomiting, and hair loss. Then, *low blood counts, pink urine, mouth sores, heart damage, nail beds may change color and texture.*

While that was dripping into me through my IV, an older lady wearing leopard-print glasses on a chain came in to give me more pieces of paper. These were about teen meetings and outings, a Southern California teen support group, and Teen Survivor's Day at Griffith Park. The lady was nice enough, but I wondered why they didn't send a teen to talk to teens about teens. Not that all of us teens loved each other so much just because we had teenness in common, but still.

The third chemo went okay.

I asked the non-teen volunteer if she had an ink pen she could spare, and she did! And it was blue! A blue Bic, which was my next choice after Paper Mate. But then Cathy said she had to find another vein to put the *bad* chemo in, and I stopped caring about paper or pens or ladies with leopard-print glasses.

Cathy said the bad one had to go into my *hand* because the veins were closer to the surface there, and it would be easier for her to see if it slipped out of the vein and into the tissue. She took out the needle in my arm and stabbed a fresh one into my hand, near my thumb.

I hoped maybe the bad chemo, DTIC, wasn't really as horrible as I'd remembered. The sheet on it did say *pain at injection*, but that sounded so mild compared to how I remembered it. Maybe the pain had been a first-time thing. And it could've been exaggerated in my memory, right?

The other possible side effects were *darkening and peeling of the skin, especially hands, dark rings in the nail beds, fever, chills, mouth sores. Nausea and vomiting* (of course) and *hair loss*, but most interesting were *scarring and stiffening of the lungs and trouble breathing*.

Cathy began pushing, and I knew instantly that it hadn't been exaggerated in my memory. If anything, it was worse than I'd remembered. With each tiny push, I felt my arm burst into flames and explode—over and over and over. I'd suck at being a spy. If I could've made the torture stop by spilling state secrets, I absolutely would have.

Cathy was very patient about going slowly. And she was still uncomplaining many hours later, when all the other beds were empty and, one by one, each of the televisions had gone quiet.

People wearing plastic aprons came by to empty the trash. I heard the janitor's floor-washing machine in the hall.

Mom was still holding on to me, trying to keep conversation alive with Cathy but too anxious and exhausted to make much sense. Dad was tipped against the wall, asleep, with his mouth open.

I was trying not to scream out loud.

We'd come in at nine o'clock that morning and staggered out to the dark, deserted parking lot at eight.

My first puke was a fairly spectacular one, half in and half out the car window, about two blocks past the Vista Theater.

{ NINE }

mom climbed into bed with me and manned the pink puke pail. I let her leave only to pee. She wanted to turn on the light at night and open the blinds in the day, but I couldn't stand it. My activities were sleeping, puking, and moaning in the dark. I kept expecting to see my insides plop into the pail, and I was amazed that my eyeballs hadn't squeezed out. I hated everything. Even Pupkin pissed me off.

I heard my brother outside my room one day or night whine to Dad, "The whole house stinks, and she woke me ten times last night with her barfing. Can't you make the hospital keep her?"

Aunt Lucy suggested music and headphones. Dad tried to show me old W. C. Fields and Marx Brothers movies, but they all gave me instant headaches.

Dad called Heather and got new antinausea drugs, which didn't work. Finally, they gave me Ativan, my old friend from the biopsy—happy juice in pill form, which Mom smashed in applesauce for me. Ativan made me *care* a lot less, but it didn't make me *puke* any less.

"ta-da! here it is!" Kay announced, holding up a gift-wrapped box with a yellow bow. "Amanda's movie. I bet it totally reeks."

My dad made popcorn for everybody else, and instant mashed potatoes for me. We gathered in the living room.

"Hey, Izz-a-smell, it's not going to bother you to see Jared, is it?" Kay asked. "Because he's probably the star."

I said, "Nah," and meant it. But I wondered if that boy, Andy, from fifth hour would be in it. I hoped so.

Kay couldn't wait to make fun of it. Mom was looking forward to being touched by it. My brother was crazy about anything on any screen, and my dad loved popcorn, so everyone was happy. I started to doze off as soon as Max hit the lights, but Kay elbowed me awake.

And there on the screen was a wobbly close-up of the words To Isabella, written on a sheet of paper. Maybe spelling my name wrong was part of the humor.

Then Jared was standing there, with balloons shoved under his shirt as huge, lopsided boobs. He was trying to keep a straight face. Whoever was holding the camera—Amanda?—shook with laughter, and you could hear her giggles in the background.

A jerk named Emmett held up a sheet of paper that said DOCTOR on it. He walked up to Jared and said, "You've got breast cancer."

Jared nodded.

Then Emmett took out a red Sharpie and *wham!* *wham!* popped both of Jared's boobs.

My brother laughed.

My mom gasped.

"That'll be ten thousand dollars, please," Emmett said, sticking out his hand.

Dad must've hit *stop* on the remote—the picture froze.

"Hey! I was watching that!" Max yelled.

"That's possibly the most tasteless thing I've ever seen in my life," Mom said.

Dad was on his feet, reaching to take out the disc. "These are *friends* of yours?" he spat.

Kay's mouth was hanging open. She was unblinking.

"I want to see the rest," I said.

"Yeah!" Max cheered. "Turn it back on! Me and Lizard want to see the rest!"

"Izzy, you don't have to subject yourself to . . . ," Mom said. "There's no reason for such—"

"I want to see it," I repeated.

"Why?" Dad asked.

"I just do."

Dad looked from me to Mom to Kay, who was still wide-eyed and speechless.

"Are you sure?" Dad asked.

I nodded. "Positive."

He didn't sit back down, but he did hit the *play* button.

We watched Jared reach into his pocket and hand Emmett a stack of Monopoly money.

Next, there were two people wearing Halloween skull masks. Jared and Emmett, I guess. Jared held a sign saying CANCER. Emmett's said CHEMO. Jared held up his hand in an imitation of the *Lone Ranger*'s version of a Native American and grunted, "How! Kemo sabe." I guess that was a pun on "chemo-sobby," but who knows? Then they threw down their signs and started fighting.

Max thought that was hilarious.

After they'd wrestled on the grass awhile, they stood up and bowed, so I guess that bit was over.

Amanda came on next, wearing a dollar-store wig. "I have cancer," she announced. This time, Emmett, still in his Grim Reaper mask, took out scissors. "Here's some chemo," he said, unable to control his giggles. Then he started hacking away at Amanda's wig.

Not even Max laughed that time.

The three of them bowed and then the skit part was over. The rest of the show was jittery out-of-focus kids in the hall saying, "Feel better, Isabelle!" and "Get well soon!"

When it was over, we all stayed where we were. Finally, Kay broke the silence, saying, "I hate them all. But mostly I hate Amanda and hope she gets her own special cancer real soon."

"Kay," Mom gasped. "What a thing to say." But her voice lacked its usual moral outrage.

Dad sat back down, looking deflated, and said, "Maybe I just don't understand kids today."

"It was lame," Max said. "Let's watch *The Simpsons*."

i started dreading the third round of chemo as soon as I'd stopped puking from the second one. By then, I was as bald as a green egg. Even my eyebrows and eyelashes were gone. Plus, I never really felt right. I was no longer turning inside out over the puke pail, but I was a little carsick, a little dizzy, and a little sore and swollen all the time. And I'd *always* rather be sleeping.

"Come on, Izz," Kay said, waking me one afternoon. "Let's go to Vroman's; my mom'll drive."

"Nooo," I whined. "I don't want to."

"Do it for me," Kay said. "I can't stand the sight of these four walls another second."

"You go, then," I said, letting my eyes close.

"No!" Kay barked. "Get up!"

I did. It took an enormous amount of effort to get dressed and find both shoes and tie them.

Kay's mom was in the kitchen, watching my mother bleach the grout between the tiles. Kay's mom's gigantic smile was in place, and I realized this was her first time seeing me bald. I had on a hat, but only a full burka or an over-the-head ski mask could've hidden all the baldness sticking out the bottom.

"Okay then!" Mom said, trying to sound normal and chipper, as if I was forever dashing off to do normal things with my friends. "Have fun, girls!"

"Fun, fun, fun," I grumbled.

Kay and I got in the backseat and I was carsick in no time. That was one of my new tricks. "If you've got to throw up, you can use this," Kay offered, opening her purse wide. I saw her hairbrush and wallet in there.

"I could use my hat," I offered. But I knew Kay's mom would probably freak if I flashed my hundred-watt head.

Kay's mom smiled at me in her rearview mirror. "Do you want me to pull over?" she asked, as if that, too, sounded fun.

I said no, and assured her and Kay and myself that I was fine, and I was. Sometimes I think the fear of being carsick is the most sickening part.

Vroman's is a massive independent bookstore in Pasadena. In the days BC (Before Cancer), Kay and I would order chai lattes and people-watch in Vroman's cafe, then wander around for hours, finding books or pictures or cartoons to show each other. If either of us had money, we'd debate endlessly over which books or magazines to actually *buy*. We always pretended everything we bought was a gift because they had cool wrapping paper and wrapped for free, if you asked.

This time, Kay and I tried to do the normalish things, but it didn't work. And as weird as *I* felt in public, Kay seemed to feel even weirder. I thought she was going to gun down everyone in the cafe, for either *looking* at me, or *not* looking at me. It was almost funny, but not quite.

Ever since Amanda's movie, I'd wondered on and off if it was possible for *any* cancer humor to be funny. So after our lattes, I went upstairs to the kids' section.

The girl with two long brown braids at the desk said, "Hi. Can I help you?"

"Do you have any joke books about cancer?" I asked. "Particularly kids with cancer?"

"You're insane," Kay hissed. "I'm serious. You're going to give her a heart attack!"

But the braid girl didn't have a heart attack, she just typed something into her computer and said, "Let's see what we have." Then she started reading off titles and short descriptions to me. Some were novels about moms and grandmothers with breast cancer. One had an older brother with bone cancer. Most were about kids dealing with their sister's or friend's or brother's illnesses and deaths.

One of her braids slipped onto the keyboard, and the salesgirl flicked it over her shoulder in annoyance. I practically felt the light thud of the braid hitting my back, as if it were mine.

Kay looked ready to burst. "Do you have any books where the kid *survives?*" she asked, as if everything were this poor salesgirl's fault.

"Let's check," the girl said. I followed her braids, hypnotized by their movement. She led us over to a corner and pulled books off the shelf to read their jackets with us. If she noticed that I was wearing a hat or didn't have hair or eyebrows, she didn't let on.

"Here's one about a kid whose experimental cancer treatment gives him super powers!" she said. That made me laugh, but it was for little kids.

After she apologized about there being no cancer joke books, she asked if we needed help with anything else.

"*Else?*" Kay snorted like a total brat.

When the salesgirl headed back to her desk, I kicked Kay. "You're acting nuts," I said. "You *so* need to get a grip!"

But Kay just got madder. "You sound like my dad! What is it with you people? Can't anyone ever *feel* anything without being called crazy?"

I walked away and Kay followed me, still barking at my heels about how crazy she wasn't.

I went to the art books, pulled a bunch off the shelf to look at, and sat down on the floor. Kay sat near me but didn't look at anything. She just held her head in her hands.

My, hasn't this been fun.

After a while, Kay's mom found us. "Time to go, girls!" she said, grinning, of course.

I went to the counter to pay for a small book of Frida Kahlo postcards, and there was Andy Siegel. I'd never noticed how tall he was. My first reaction was to duck behind the rack of designer bookmarks until he was gone. But Kay just got in line behind him without a thought and said, "Hey, don't you go to our school?"

Andy turned around. "Yeah," he said. Then he saw me and smiled. Maybe it was an, *Oh! Time to smile at the cancer kid* smile, but maybe not.

"So you skip class but still make it to Vroman's," he said. "I'm telling." He glanced down at the book in my hand. I held up one of Frida's self-portraits, with her gory heart and severed arteries on the outside of her body. It was wonderfully gruesome.

"I figure these will make nice thank-you cards for all my get-well gifts," I said, and Andy laughed. Not an embarrassed, awkward, phony-assed laugh, but a laugh like he got it, like he got *me*.

Kay looked from me to him and back again. I could see her brain ticking away, and I almost put my hand over her mouth before she blurted out something stupid. But she didn't.

The person in front of Andy left. We all moved up in line. And there on the counter, next to the mini reading lights, was one of those cardboard fund-raiser things with slots for coins. This one had a picture of a smiling bald kid in a red baseball cap and the words *Leukemia Lymphoma Society of Southern California* across the top.

"Hey! That's my disease!" I said, pointing. "But why are so many of the holes empty? Lazy greed-heads can't spare a donation?" Not that I myself ever forked over any quarters, but still.

The bearded guy behind the counter rang up Andy's stuff, looking a little embarrassed.

"Then again," I said, trying to act a little less wacko, "what's a stinking quarter going to do?"

Andy got his change and put fifty cents in the slots. "But *two* stinking quarters is a whole different story!" he said.

"I'm cured!" I cheered.

Andy put up his hand for a high five, and we grinned at each other while I paid for my Frida postcards.

"See you at school?" he asked.

"I suppose, now that I'm cured, I'll have no choice," I answered.

Andy laughed, and headed for the door. He saluted both me and Kay, saying, "See ya."

We answered, "See ya," in unison, and I turned to see Kay with her eyes bugged out. That *really* cracked me up.

When her shock had worn off a little and we were back in the car, she said, "Well, you should totally thank me for dragging you out of the house today so you could flirt your brains out with that guy."

"Andy," I said.

"Whatever."

But then, Kay's mom swerved so nauseatingly around a corner that the dry heaves wiped Andy out of my mind.

back to Children's for chemo number three.

As soon as we got off the freeway, I started to gag. The sign for the *live nude girls* and all the other familiar sites made me woozy. The smell of the hospital parking lot, the Benadryl stink in the stairwell, the painted lady-bug, the orange stickers, the green-and-white striped mask—all of it made me feel crappy.

This time, I didn't want to do *anything* while we waited for the results of the blood work. I sat on one of the gray chairs and stared at the wall. Maybe I fell asleep, I'm not sure. There was the usual ongoing parade of misery, but I didn't care.

I looked up once and recognized that guy who had wanted to play Candy Land. He still had his hair. I almost said something to get his attention, but what was there to say? He'd probably never recognize me now anyway, and I really didn't care. I closed my eyes and let myself drift. It occurred to me that I'd joined the ranks of the seriously gorked. Now I was one of those zombie kids just waiting to die—but so what?

I flunked my blood test and they sent me home. I was relieved but too tired to celebrate. The chemo was post-poned, but not canceled, and no matter how I looked at it, I had six more rounds to go. Six had never seemed such an impossibly huge number till now.

I slept the next few days but dragged myself to school on Friday.

On the bus, Melinda Kramer turned around in her seat to tell me that her grandfather had cancer.

I smiled at Melinda and said, "And he died, right?"

She nodded.

Trevor Nelson leaned across the aisle and added, "Mine did, too."

"Thanks for sharing, guys," I said sweetly.

They both smiled at me, but then Melinda squinted suspiciously and turned her back. Trevor started playing "Stairway to Heaven" on air guitar.

When I got to school and found Kay, I told her about the bus conversation. She got way angrier than necessary and wanted to go beat the crap out of both of them.

"Lighten up!" I told Kay. "It wasn't a big deal. It was just dumb. Actually, I thought it was a little funny."

Kay fumed.

"I don't know," I said. "I think saying the wrong thing beats saying nothing at all."

But Kay was beyond reach. I was beginning to miss her.

I tried to be the Izzy Miller that I was before, but I couldn't remember how. And it was exhausting to try. Not just with Kay, but with everyone. Everything seemed so screamingly irrelevant. How could I get all twisted by the stupid things those idiots said on the bus? I couldn't get mad at that stuff any more than I could be thrilled by letters from kids who didn't know me.

And it was the same with everything else—how could I possibly care about Algebra *now* when I never did before?

Screw it! I thought. I'll deal with all this later, one thing at a time. Cancer now, the rest of it—*not* now.

I was a teeny-tiny bit curious to see Andy Siegel, but that seemed dumb. Plus, there was no way I could push through to fifth period, and he wasn't in any of my classes until then.

I didn't think I could even face the lunch scene, so after second period, I called Aunt Lucy to pick me up. She always wanted to be the one who understood me better than my mom, so I knew she'd get there fast, and she did.

I'd never been particularly girlie, even when I had hair, and now I really looked gender-neutral, but Aunt

Lucy ignored my objections and whisked me off to high tea in a very frilly, ultrafem tea shop in Burbank. We sat at a table with a lace tablecloth and cloth napkins. The china was delicate, the silver was silver, and the teapot wore a cozy.

I carefully nibbled tiny crustless sandwiches and scones, trying to avoid my mouth sores. Aunt Lucy guzzled tea.

"Now what's wrong?" she asked.

I took off my hat.

"Oh," she said, reaching out to touch my bald green head. "Bad hair day?"

"I'm not cut out for this," I said. "I'm just no good at it."

"At being bald?"

"Yeah, and everything else. Being bald and a good sport and trying to act normal and not freak out, or freak anyone else out. The Moon Child is supposed to be all brave and sweet and angelic. That's how she is in the movies."

"Well, you're not auditioning for the role," Aunt Lucy said. "It's just about getting through it—however you can."

"Well, I *hate* it! I hate everything about it. Everything!"

"Of course you do!" Aunt Lucy said. "It's entirely hateful. And you're entitled to throw as big a tantrum as you like, as often as you like." She swallowed the last of her tea and handed me her cup. It had a pink rosebud pattern.

"Would you like to throw this, Izzy?" she asked. "Feel free, it comes with the price of tea. Perhaps through the window? That might be satisfying."

I put the cup down on the table. "I'd still have cancer, though," I said.

"True enough," she said "But less and less with each session of chemotherapy. Just push through all this and you can come out the other side and start your life all over."

"But everyone is so incredibly irritating," I said.

"Well, cancer or not, *that'll* never change," Aunt Lucy laughed. "But for that, there's always chocolate!" She held up one of the tiny chocolate tea biscuits and popped it in her mouth. Her eyes closed in ecstasy. Then she said, "Thank goodness!"

that Monday was attempt number two at chemo number three.

This time, the drive didn't just make me woozy, it made me puke. And puke again in the stairwell at the first whiff of hospital.

I got Cathy as my chemo nurse again, and she said a lot of older kids have the same reaction. "Programmed response," she said while she draped a sheet over the IV pole, making it look like a ghost. She examined my arms and hands and told me the scarring was bad and that some of my veins were shot.

"Meaning, shot *forever*?"

"Maybe not," Cathy said. "Sometimes, after a while . . ." Then she shrugged. "How did it go after your last treatment?" she asked.

"Awful," I said.

She nodded, as if that was to be expected.

"I barfed for days, and was dizzy and stupid, with a splitting headache," I added.

Cathy nodded again. "Let's try something different this time," she said. "I'll order some Ativan to start. It's an anti-anxiety."

"Ativan and I are old friends," I said. "I'm planning to name my first kid Ativan if it's a girl. Don't you think that would be pretty?"

"Uh-oh," Cathy said, "is this a drug fiend in training?"

"And you know what else sounds good, as a girl's name?" I asked. "Melanoma."

"Skin cancer?"

"No, *skin cancer* sounds awful, but *Melanoma* is pretty."

"I'm sure your daughters would really appreciate that," Cathy said. "But at a certain age, they have to hate you for *something*, so I guess it may as well be for their names."

"And how about Zofran if I have a boy?" I added. "Isn't that the antinausea drug that fizzles on your tongue?"

Cathy nodded, then said, "I never thought of Zofran as particularly male." Then back to business, she added, "Dr. Seacole put in for Marinol, if you'd like to try it. It's medical marijuana, and it helps some people with their nausea. Are you okay with that?"

"Of course," I said.

My parents added, "If it'll help, absolutely. Do anything you can."

Since I can't swallow pills, Cathy mashed the Ativan in cherry syrup. The Marinol was an oil in a rubbery round gel thing, so I just chewed it up and gagged it down.

Meanwhile, Cathy found a vein in my right arm, above my elbow, practically in my armpit. So much for drawing. I told Dad to put away my notebook and pen.

I asked Cathy, half kidding, if they ever used feet or necks, and she said yes. My neck throbbed with the thought. Then she started the first chemo and talked to my parents about her wedding plans, and other easy subjects.

I leafed through the *National Enquirer* and *Star* and *People* with my left hand, until suddenly, my brain started to sag down onto my forehead, and I had to raise my eyebrows to keep the top of my head from melting.

Cathy must've noticed my bizarre facial expressions, because right about then, she said, "I do believe the Marinol is working."

I sent my dad downstairs to McDonald's for double fries and a shake and whatever desserts they had.

"Isabelle has the munchies," Cathy said. And that cracked me up.

The bad chemo still hurt plenty, but it didn't take nearly as long. We were out of there in three and a half hours, instead of five. But I couldn't walk and had to be taken in a wheelchair to the car.

I made my parents pull over at Gelson's Market because I was starving. My legs were still gooey, so we used the market's motorized shopping cart–scooter thing. Mom rode with me. She steered, but not much better than I would have.

Wheee! I giggled hysterically, wanting almost everything on the shelves.

The other shoppers were too well behaved to stare at the green-headed stoner and the tear-streaked lady zigzagging up the aisles with a chubby bearded guy scurrying behind them picking up the things they dropped.

Back in the car, I gobbled down the deli-counter stuffed cabbage and the mac and cheese before we'd even reached the freeway. Then I ripped open a bag of marshmallows and shoved handfuls into my mouth. I washed it down with root beer, then followed that with huge hunks gouged out of the center of a cherry pie, breaking two tines off my white plastic fork.

And I kept it all down until nearly midnight, when out it came, looking very much as it had going in, the cheese, the cherries, so colorful on my sheets.

Mom fed me more Marinol every four hours. But if she waited too long and the last dose was wearing off, I'd throw up whatever she gave me. Timing was everything.

Through the front window, I heard Dad proudly tell our next-door neighbor that I'd had a two-hundred-dollar vomit.

"Hey! She could probably sell that on the street!" Martin said. "You could make a fortune selling puke to the potheads."

Ha-ha. Humor around our house had definitely changed.

{ TEN }

people came with gifts and food, and all of it whirled around me, making very little sense. I didn't mind. I dozed, I ate, I dozed again. I watched cartoons with my brother. I puked, but not as much as before. My head hurt, but not so terribly.

I lived on the living-room couch. Mom vacuumed around me. Max took his piano lesson two feet from my head. I wore an old Barbie headband to keep my forehead out of my eyes.

It got to the point that everyone would be sitting around and, when necessary, Mom would hand me the puke pail without missing a beat in the conversation. Max didn't even glance away from his *Spongebob* cartoons when I hurled within splashing distance of where he sprawled, and life went on around me as if everything were perfectly normal. My days passed in a daze.

"Do you want me to bring you your notebook?" Mom occasionally asked. But my hands were too screwed up to hold a pen, and I didn't have the brainpower to draw, anyway. Once in a while, I'd think of something that might make a good drawing, but the thought of actually doing it seemed like way too much trouble.

"Look what Aunt Lucy brought!" Mom announced, holding up a box of blue Paper Mate medium points and a fresh new spiral notebook. But the urge was gone. Those days were over.

every now and then, they dragged me to the cardiology department of Children's to see if the chemo was destroying my heart. That would figure, I thought, if I was killed by the cure. At least there were no needles or pokes with an echocardiogram—or, as we on the inside called it, an *echo.*

kay visited after school, like an ambassador from another country, another planet. She brought schoolwork, but I didn't touch it.

"Izz," she said, "you've got to pass. I can't start high school in September all alone. You have to graduate and come with me."

I told her to stop bugging me.

Kay rattled the notes and study guides she'd brought. "Please?" she begged. "It's not like you're doing anything else but sitting around on your big butt, stoned out of your gourd."

"Big?" I asked. "Did you call me *fat?*"

"Okay, scrawny. Your bony, flat, nonexistent butt. Is that better?"

I pretended to pout.

Mom came in. "Kay, honey, did you wash your hands?"

eventually, I guess Mom told Heather about my refusal to go to school between chemos, and in walked Larry Rodriguez, my very own tutor.

Larry had huge blue veins twisting all around his arms and the backs of his hands. What a waste of veins, I thought jealously. But Larry also had wonderfully low academic expectations of me, and that was good. Mostly he rattled on about his pitiful life as an actor, his auditions and disappointments.

Sometimes I listened harder than others; it didn't seem to matter to him either way. I guess *any* audience was better than none.

Larry thought the best thing for me would be to have contact with other kids who were going through similar hells. I tried to tell him that we were too busy going through it to give a shit about anyone else, but he insisted. He came in one morning, deliriously happy with himself for finding a cancer teens Web site for me. I admit, I was a little curious about whether other kids felt the same churning anger and hopelessness that I felt all day and all night, so I let him show me.

The first blog I read was by a guy named Gabe, who had a brain tumor. He talked about the whole thing in military terms; the cancer was his enemy, but he was sure he'd be victorious in his battle. And he believed that the worst thing would be to give up fighting.

I wasn't even sure what he meant. Was I fighting just by sticking out my arm and letting nurses squeeze poison into me? Wasn't that kind of *passive* for a soldier?

The thought of all that fighting and marching was so exhausting, my eyes closed.

"Here's one!" Larry chirped, jarring me awake.

That one was by a girl named Danielle with pancreatic cancer, who felt grateful for all the things she had learned about herself since her diagnosis. She said she thought of it not as a *sickness*, but as a *journey of self-discovery*.

"That's truly amazing!" Larry said, poking the computer screen with his stubby index finger. "It's *so* like the theater! Acting is *all* about the journey. I *knew* there was a profound connection between myself and the children I tutor."

My brain, doped and sluggish as it was, went through a million replies, but settled at last on, "Whatever."

The third one was another boy, Joshua, and his was all about God and prayer and faith and trust in His will and being tested and being pure of heart.

I wished all three of them well. I really did hope Gabe won his war and Danielle enjoyed her journey and Josh either got God to reconsider or prayed himself into a happy place—whatever got them through. But I didn't have the stomach to read a fourth blog, and Larry finally stopped nagging.

one morning, my dad came into the living room with his coffee and sat at the foot of my couch. His hair was still sleep-styled, and his eyes were lumpy. He said, "I get up and get dressed, and go out there every morning as if I were still the same. It's amazing how life works."

I wasn't sure what we were talking about, but I could tell it was deep.

"When you were little, I could blow away your pains with a puff. Do you remember that?" he asked.

I waited for him to go on.

"You'd announce, 'Owie!' And hold up your finger or your knee for me to blow on. And *poof*! That's all it took."

I nodded.

"What magic breath I had."

I laughed.

"I don't recall feeling smug or heroic. I'd just get dressed and go to work each morning, exactly as I do now. I must've assumed I'd always be able to blow away my little Izzy-pie's pain."

"It's okay, Daddy," I said. "I know you still would if you could."

He shook his head and said, "I took my powers for granted."

I repeated, "It's okay, Daddy," hoping he wouldn't start to cry. I could take Mom's tears 24-7, but there was no way in hell I could handle my dad's.

one time, Mom was out filling my prescriptions, so I answered the phone. Usually I let the machine pick up because the way people asked me how I was feeling always made me feel worse. But this time, I'd just been talking to my aunt Lucy, and the phone rang in my hand. Answering it was a reflex.

"Hello?"

"Isabelle? Is that you?"

"Yes."

"Oh, my, you sound so grown up! This is Patty Michaels, from Glendale Community School? Remember? I'm Natalie's mother?"

Community was my preschool, and the only thing I remembered about it was that they wouldn't let me eat my Rice Krispies Treat because it was made with processed sugar.

I said, "Hi."

"Isabelle, dear," the mom said, "I heard about your illness, and we all just want you to know that we're thinking positive thoughts for you."

"Okay."

"And I was wondering if I could bring Natalie and maybe a few of your other friends from Community by for a visit?"

And that, I think, was when I hit bottom, the lowest low of the whole stinking disease—that second, trapped on the phone with some lady who wanted to bring over a bunch of girls I didn't remember, to look at me.

I could see this chick shaking her finger and telling her SUV full of spoiled girls that I was an example of what *real* problems were. That they should take a good, long look at my bald head, my scarred-up arms, et cetera, and thank the Lord they weren't me.

I'd be today's lesson on why they should be grateful for everything they had and stop whining for more clothes or more spending money or whatever.

I pretended I was on a cell and it was breaking up. When the phone rang again, I ignored it.

Later, my mom said, "Izzy! You'll never guess who called! It was the sweetest thing—"

I cut her off before she could mention that woman's name. "This is not the cancer channel," I said. "There will be no show!"

"Oh, Izzy, I don't know why you choose to see everything in such a negative light," Mom said. "I'm sure Patty Mi—"

"Don't say that name or I'll scream!" I said. "I swear!"

Mom shook her head, sighed, and dropped the subject.

unlike Larry, who worships his own image and did his tiny bits of teaching directly to his reflection in the window behind my couch, I avoided mirrors and reflective surfaces. But sometimes, I'd slip up and catch a glance. The serious girl peering in at me from the dark window or out of the oven door or the blank computer screen—the hollow, sunken eyes wiggling up through the shine on the coffee table—was like those pictures of haunted-looking people in concentration camps, bald, gray-skinned, skeletal, with cracked lips.

Sometimes, I half thought about what my self-portrait would look like, and once I even went as far as reaching for a pen. But the mood passed quickly, and the pen fell out of my hand.

by the sixth chemo, I no longer saw the point.

I hurt all over, all the time, and my brain was mush. I had no real life. I couldn't remember ever having one in the past or picture ever having one in the future. And I couldn't imagine caring about it, anyway.

"Just three more," my mom said. "You're more than halfway done!"

But I couldn't think of reasons to go through the whole chemo nightmare three more times. Nothing seemed worth that much pain.

If one more well-meaning person told me it was *normal* or *okay* to be depressed, as if I needed anyone's *permission*, as if there were anything even remotely *normal* about my existence, I would have killed them, if I'd had the energy.

And I knew, in my heart, that the chemo wasn't working—no one could feel the way I felt and be *getting better*.

Bad times.

Really bad times.

Pupkin put his big head in my lap and I could swear he was saying good-bye.

But I didn't quit the chemo. I didn't have the strength. I got in the car when I was told to. I stuck out my arm when I was asked to. I threw up when I had to, and I slept when I could.

My birthday came and I blew out the candles. But when Kay told me to make a wish, it took me a while to think of one.

i was on the couch under a pile of blankets when Kay came in wearing a tank top, shorts, and flip-flops.

"That's just pathetic!" she said. "It's like a million degrees out, and look at you!"

"Shut up," I mumbled.

"You shut up. And take off that stupid blanket. What you need is some sun on that fish-belly skin of yours," Kay said, pulling off my blankets like Mom used to do in the old days. "Now get up!"

I crabbed and grumbled to my feet. Then I staggered out the back door to stand blinking in the glaring sunlight.

"God, you're like some underground grub-thing," Kay said. "I can't believe I let it go on so long! Straighten up!" she added, poking my shoulder blades.

My dad was on his knees, weeding the flowerbed. I wondered how he could tell the weeds from the flowers. My cancer was my weeds. It didn't throw its head back and cackle *muahahaha* or rub its hands with glee, plotting my destruction. It was just trying to live, like the weeds, with no evil intent.

"What do you care if there are weeds?" I asked Dad.

"They fight with the flowers for sun and water and root space," he explained.

"Well," I said, shielding my eyes in the light and wobbling a bit on my shaky legs, "why don't you let them work it out themselves?"

Dad kept weeding and answered as if he were talking to the plants. "Because if I don't help them, the flowers will lose for sure. The weeds are stronger than they are."

"But why do you have to pick sides?" I asked.

Dad sat back and looked at me. "Because it's my yard. And I want flowers," he said.

Off to the side, I thought I saw Kay wipe her eyes. I looked over and sure enough, there were tears.

"What?" I asked, unable to hide my annoyance.

Kay ducked a little and flicked her hair to hide her face. "It's all so violent," she said, defensively. "Even the plants have to fight for their lives."

"Don't start acting like my mom," I warned. "Just *don't*." But it was too late. In that one second, I realized with horror that even Kay expected me to lose out to the weeds, eventually.

Even Kay.

She tried to change the subject, poked me in the back again, and barked at me to stand up straight.

I turned to crawl back inside. "Leave me alone," I said, heading for the couch. "I'm really tired."

I lay down and closed my eyes, knowing Kay would give up soon and go away. I also knew she'd feel terrible if she knew I was on to her. But I didn't have the strength to pretend. Funny, I thought, that it had never even occurred to me that Kay thought I'd die. I'd always just assumed she believed in me.

Funny, too, I realized, with an icy chill in my gut, that it had never really occurred to *me* that I might die from this. It hadn't been positive thinking, exactly, more like stubbornness. Lack of imagination. Denial.

Sure enough, Kay soon tiptoed away, thinking I was asleep. But after school the next day, she was back.

"That's it!" she said. "Enough is enough. We have to whip you into shape for graduation." She was dead set on my wearing a cap and gown and graduating with the class. It became Kay's obsession, and she was a total pain in the ass about it.

"You're like a fly," I said, trying to bat her away. But she kept nagging.

I tried to explain to her how far away and unconnected I felt to that old part of my life, but she wouldn't let up. I told her that if my blood had never failed, and I'd done every chemo exactly two weeks apart as planned, I could've graduated from the chemotherapy, and maybe the cancer, at the same time that school ended. "*All that* might have seemed worth celebrating," I said. "But not just school."

Kay snorted.

Eventually, I was too worn down to fight. So, on June 16, just to shut her up, I let her put a ton of makeup on my pale, puffy face. We picked out my tackiest hat— pink with plastic fruit and dyed feathers—and went to the damn graduation.

It wasn't so bad. I'd forgotten that I ever knew all those kids, but I'd been in school with some of them since kindergarten. I saw Jared with Amanda and avoided them so I wouldn't have to say anything about their piece-of-shit movie. I wondered if they'd expected thanks. Kay and I found Penelope and Mica and Becca, and we all clumped together like the old friends we were.

I found myself looking around and finally admitted to myself that I was hunting for Andy Siegel. I didn't have to look far, though, because he was class valedictorian, and got up to give a speech. Luckily, he didn't recite an overly patriotic, nauseatingly school-spirited collection of cliché's—like the class president did—so I didn't have to hate him. Good. I really didn't want to have to hate Andy, not one single bit.

It was unbelievably hot out, with no shade anywhere. I squinted at the limp crowd baking on folding chairs, fanning themselves with programs. I bet Andy's sister was somewhere sweating in the audience. I didn't see anyone wearing a tiara.

I knew the standing ovation when they called my name was for the *cancer kid*, not for *me*. But still, applause is applause, so I took a bow. When I sneaked a peek at Andy, he was grinning from head to toe and looking right at me. I was almost completely positive it wasn't a cancer grin.

Mom cried her eyes out, of course, and even Aunt Lucy looked a little pinkish around the nose. My dad must've taken fifty pictures.

Max said my hat was ugly and that I looked dumb in that stupid robe.

"Aw, shucks, kid," I said. "I love you, too."

then a few days after the last puke of the last chemo, it was time to get the comparison scan. Six months, half a year, had limped and shuffled past since that first morning in the bathroom. The lumps in my neck that had started it all were long gone. One had been cut out for the biopsy, and the other disappeared after the very first chemo. That meant the chemotherapy had worked at least *some*. I tried not to think about what they'd do to me next if it hadn't worked entirely.

Dad took the day off. Max was sent to Riley's. Mom was still on a leave-of-absence from work. Aunt Lucy met us at the hospital and brought Kay as a surprise. I don't know where they told Kay's dad they were going, but I bet anything, he didn't know it was the hospital.

I didn't really get the point of all this since it was just the scan and we wouldn't get the results right away, but if they all felt they needed to be there, fine.

I watched the dots assemble on the computer monitor, inching up my body. I wasn't sure what I was looking for, but I figured I'd recognize trouble if I saw it. In the end, though, it just looked like dots. The test took an hour and a half, and I left feeling unsure.

Afterward, we all went to lunch at *La Belle Epoch*. Everyone tried to act festive and optimistic, toasting our cups of soda and coffee to my getting a perfect scan. It was exhausting and I felt like hell. My poor old body had been through so much, I doubted it would ever forgive me.

then the wait for Heather's call began. I told my dad I wouldn't want her job unless the news was always good, which it couldn't be.

"But even if the news is bad," Dad said, "it doesn't mean it's hopeless. It just means they have to try something else. That's all."

By the next afternoon, Dad was spouting more facts and statistics than ever, about how if it turned out that I had to get radiation next, that would be good too. *Wagga* percent of cases do well after *wagga* number of extra doses of chemo, plus radiation or whatever, with no recurrence.

Mom was a mess. She jumped whenever the phone rang. And even though we had call-waiting and she knew she'd get beeped if it was Heather, Mom hung up, *bam!* on anyone who dared call. The second or third time she slammed down the phone on someone, she hissed, "*Damn* them!"

"Yes!" I laughed. "Finally!"

heather called just a few minutes after Kay walked in the door. In fact, all Kay'd had time to do was take off her shoes and greet Pupkin.

I nabbed the phone before Mom got it.

"Your scan was clear," Heather said. "Congratulations, Isabelle, you are cancer-free."

"What?" I said, making her repeat it, in case I was hallucinating. Mom, meanwhile, had my arm in a vice grip and was searching my face frantically for clues. There was a split second's temptation to mess with everyone's minds, but I don't think I could've kept from smiling if I tried.

All hell broke loose. Kay leapt about twenty feet in the air, then jumped around screaming like a total lunatic, while Dad grabbed me and Mom in a mammoth dad-hug. He laughed a big, Santa-like *ho-ho-ho*—his happy belly shaking the rest of us. And Mom, of course, blubbered uncontrollably.

My brother called Aunt Lucy and screamed, "Lizard isn't dying!" into the phone at her.

"i never believed you had cancer in the first place," Max told me later that night.

And I confessed to him, "Neither did I."

i'm in art school now. I've branched out a bit and use oil pastels and paints, although I've always got a spiral notebook handy, and a medium-point blue Paper Mate pen stuck in my long, braided *hair*. Hair, I might add, that I've never cut since my days as a Moon Child.

My parents survived my cancer and are going about their lives more or less like normal people. Kay is doing great, working her ass off in premed. She says she's thinking of going into pediatric oncology. I wonder where she got that idea? And Andy and I have been going out for ages. He's as sweet and funny as ever; my brother, Max, worships him.

I still have to get scans once in a while, but hey, everyone has *some* shit in their life, right?